# SONG AND DANCE

Rosemary Brooke is picked out of a third-rate nightclub by Dane Goodman, a highly successful composer, to be the leading lady in his new production. After working her almost to breaking point, he takes her to his house above Cannes to recuperate, where they fall in love. On their return to London, Rosemary distances herself from Dane when he questions her about her family. What is the mystery which she tries so hard to keep buried?

*Books by Alix Malcolm*
*in the Linford Romance Library:*

FALCON'S LURE

ALIX MALCOLM

# SONG AND DANCE

*Complete and Unabridged*

**LINFORD**
*Leicester*

First published in Great Britain in 1991 by
Robert Hale Limited
London

First Linford Edition
published 1998
by arrangement with
Robert Hale Limited
London

British Library CIP Data

Malcolm, Alix
    Song and dance.—Large print ed.—
Linford romance library
1. Love stories
2. Large type books
I. Title
823.9′14 [F]

ISBN 0–7089–5356–5

Published by
F. A. Thorpe (Publishing) Ltd.
Anstey, Leicestershire

Set by Words & Graphics Ltd.
Anstey, Leicestershire
Printed and bound in Great Britain by
T. J. International Ltd., Padstow, Cornwall

This book is printed on acid-free paper

# 1

The dark smoky atmosphere had Dane Goodman grimacing in distaste. He turned to his companion,

'They'd better be good, Paul! This is the last time I'm going to allow you to drag me around like this. So far this evening I've endured four hours of purgatory; been forced to drink indifferent wine; had my ears assaulted by so-called music, and I think my digestion's going to be permanently impaired!'

'Don't blame me! You're the one who's looking for the perfect girl . . . If the top agents in London can't satisfy you, then you've got to be prepared to tour the provinces!'

'I'm not going through this agony again! You can do all the preliminary work in future, and if you think you've found anything then I'll come and have a look . . . My God what a life!' He looked around him, hardly troubling to keep his scorn hidden as he looked at the people at the nearby tables waiting for the cabaret to begin. 'You must be mad to think that we'll find anything any good here!'

'I don't agree with you!' Paul answered sharply. 'This club has won quite a little reputation for helping talented youngsters on their way!'

Dane Goodman shut his eyes. Judging by the expression of pain on his face it was obvious that he wished he could shut his ears as well. The compère came on to announce the next act.

'Ladies and gentlemen! Let's hear you for some of the prettiest songbirds you're ever likely to see! And, boy! Can they move as well? The Love-birds!'

The spotlights shifted onto five girls, who started to sing and dance to one of the current pop songs. Paul risked a glance at Dane, but he was still sitting with his eyes shut, an expression of boredom on his face. Ignoring him, he allowed his eyes to assess the girls. They could certainly all dance, but it was hard to tell about their voices against the background noise. The girl in the middle interested him the most; the reason he had dragged Dane down to the club. She was due to sing a solo, and if she was as good as he had been told, then maybe this would be the end of their search.

When she started to sing he sat back in his chair and relaxed for the first time that evening. There was no doubt about it, the girl had star quality. It didn't matter that the material chosen was banal, or that her performance was amateurish; these were faults that could be corrected. She had that certain something that his years in show business had taught him was more important than any act. A quality that could catch and hold your attention. He was not surprised to see that Dane was alert, with that peculiarly watchful expression he wore when he was interested. 'Not bad?' he mouthed, a glimmer of hope in his heart that the long search might soon be over.

'That was one of the most appalling displays I've ever had to sit through!' was the discouraging return. He had chosen to speak as the clapping was dying down, his voice loud enough to be heard a considerable way from their table. His voice was lower as he continued: 'All the same, I think you could be right. That dark one; I'd like to hear her sing properly. Get in touch with their agent, if they've got one!' Again his voice sounded scornful, 'and let me know when you've set it up. Now, let's get the hell out of here, I can't stand another minute . . . '

'Hey, Romy!' Backstage in the girls' dressing-room, the leggy redhead's face was full of mischief and something else as she spoke to the dark girl who sang the solo. 'You know who that was out front tonight?'

Rosemary Brooke smeared cleansing cream over her face before answering. 'You mean Dane Goodman and Paul

Saint? Yes, I saw them, and heard Goodman's comment on our act!' she finished drily.

The redhead pursed her mouth in mock disappointment. 'Didn't you mind? He's supposed to be searching for a new star for his latest musical, but that was a pretty damning thumbs-down for you, wasn't it?'

Romy shrugged her shoulders carelessly. 'I never believe gossip, so unlike you I wasn't expecting a sudden rise to stardom! But I'm sorry they've disappointed you . . . '

The other girls laughed at the way she had managed to put Sally in her place; they knew the redhead was jealous of her, but Romy never responded to her jibes. Sally had wanted to lead them when their previous singer had left to get married, but their manager had insisted on Romy taking the place instead of her.

'Sometimes you're just unreal!' Sally continued: 'Why don't you admit that you're just as ambitious as the rest of us to get on?'

'I do admit it!' Romy answered softly, 'but I know I've still got a lot to learn. Okay, I accept that we haven't exactly hit the big time yet, but at least we're working!'

'You'll make it one day, Romy girl!' Cleo, the oldest of the girls, turned to smile at her. 'Your dancing's all right and you can sing like an angel! I've been around long enough to recognise talent when I see it, and I don't think it will be long before your name is in lights! I'm not going to make it any further than I already have. And that's something that you're going to have to come to terms with!' She addressed her last sentence to the redhead, and, ignoring her furious face, continued: 'You'd do better to give it up and marry that young man who's so crazy about you!'

Intervening, Romy said, 'That's unfair, Cleo! Sally is the best dancer we've got!'

The older girl shrugged carelessly, 'That's not saying a lot!'

Romy was conscious of tiredness, and all she wanted to do was get away to think about what had just happened. She soon changed into her normal clothes of shabby jeans and jersey topped with an old navy reefer jacket.

It was a filthy night, wind and rain making the prospect of leaving the club an ordeal.

Luckily the boarding-house where she had a room wasn't far away, and the weather made the risk of walking back alone not quite as stupid as it appeared. Normally they never took the chance; the hours that they worked made it foolish to gamble that they wouldn't be molested. There were still, even in these enlightened days, a number of men who thought that stage performers were open for offers after hours.

With relief Romy shut the door of her room and was truly able to relax for the first time that evening. She got ready for bed, first making some hot chocolate. As she sipped the comforting drink, her mind ran back to the events of that evening.

Sally had been right; a deep and burning ambition to succeed was her only mainstay in a life that had had more than its share of unhappiness. On the death of her teacher parents a little over a year ago she had been left with only her belief in herself to keep her going. Her mother had trained her voice and encouraged her to think that one day she might be able to earn her living from it, and if what she was doing now was a far cry from what her mother had hoped for her, then at least it was a start.

She was nineteen years old, but circumstances made her seem far older. She thought she was pretty enough, but nothing special without her stage make-up. Her only true claim to beauty was her eyes. They were a light hazel, and their colour changed according to her mood. Her thick, unruly hair hung round her small face like a pony's mane if she left it loose, and small, neat features totally dominated by her large eyes. Her figure was good enough, although her bust was a trifle too large for a dancer. Looked at dispassionately in a mirror she was okay, she supposed, without being special.

What she never saw though was the way her enthusiasm had a way of lighting her up, as if someone had lit a candle inside her. It was this ability that gave her that extra something on stage. She could no more help responding to an audience than she could breathe. This evening she had sung with all her heart to the two men watching her so closely and it had been a bitter blow to hear Dane Goodman's all too audible verdict on her performance.

She was hungry for the life of a star, as if that could make up for the empty void her parents' death had left in her life.

She could see Dane Goodman's face in front of her now, the dark brown eyes lit with flecks of gold in the reflected stage lighting, and the dark curly hair above his olive skin, almost as if he had gypsy ancestry. He had looked vital and alive, as if her singing had meant something to him, so the shock of his final words had been all the greater. All at once it became of supreme importance to her to prove to him and everyone else who had doubted her that they were wrong. She would succeed one day in spite of the harsh words.

The call from her agent the next morning came therefore as a shock. Joe Manning's enthusiasm for her verged on the hysterical.

'I knew it, darling! I knew all along that you had real star quality! It's for the lead part in his newest musical. They think that you might be exactly what they have been looking for!'

'That's not what he said last night!' she answered drily. 'He thought our act was appalling and said so, very loudly indeed!'

Joe Manning brushed that aside. 'He wants to hear you in the rehearsal room at the Palace at eleven o'clock tomorrow morning. Do you want me to come along and hold your hand?'

'No! I mean it's very kind of you, Joe, but I can manage on my own.'

'I've arranged a stand-in for the rest of the week at the club. We should know by then whether you are in or not! Paul Saint told me that they were both very impressed . . . ' Romy put the phone down, torn between a mixture of emotions. Her heart was beating at twice its normal rate. This was her chance to break into the big time, but for all her elation she had the feeling that if she went for this audition she might somehow regret it.

She couldn't get out of her mind the scathing way Dane Goodman had dismissed her last night. Such behaviour had to belong to someone so arrogant that he took no account of lesser beings. He had come to dominate the musical scene in London over the last ten years with a string of hits; perhaps his success had gone to his head. There was no denying that he was exceedingly talented as a composer, his songs regularly making the charts, and his name had become synonymous with box-office success.

Standing outside the stage door the next morning she had to fight hard not to turn tail and run. The butterflies were churning in her stomach, and when she opened her mouth to give her name she had to clear her throat twice before her voice would obey her. The doorman consulted a clipboard list and Romy tried to control her quivering nerves. She took two or three deep breaths, and tried to ignore the sounds of rehearsal in the distance, the heavy beat of the music seeming to keep time with the beats of her heart. The sound of footsteps running down the stone stairs had her looking apprehensively at the curly-headed young man who came lightly to a stop in front of her.

'Hi! I'm Chips Grant, Saint Paul's

assistant you know . . . ' He stopped and grinned at her face. 'Hey, come on! You've got nothing to be afraid of, have you?'

Romy managed a stiff little smile before answering. 'Sorry! But, yes, I am a little nervous . . . '

'You don't need to be, or at least not yet! The great man hasn't arrived, he's been delayed or something, so to start with it will only be me and my boss. Can you read music, by the way?' Romy nodded her head, still not sufficiently sure of herself to trust her voice.

'You'll have time to study the music before we start. Have you seen the show yet?' Again she shook her head. 'That's terrible!' The friendly young voice went on, 'We'll have to do something about that . . . ' At last he threw open a door. 'Here we are! Number one practice room at your disposal! Can I call you Rosemary, by the way?'

She gave him her first genuine smile

of the day, 'You'd better make it Romy, everyone else does . . . '

'That's better, you're beginning to look quite human! Take off your coat and settle down, I'll get you a coffee, shall I?' Still smiling at him she nodded. 'Good! Now you're beginning to relax you can look at the music, it's on the piano.' He turned on his heel, lightly as a dancer, and left her alone.

Romy threw her coat onto one of the chairs and moved over to the piano, picking up the top sheet of music before sinking down onto the stool. Slowly she began to pick out the notes on the piano, then softly began to sing as she became more confident. She heard the door open behind her, and without turning round said, 'That was quick! Did you pull rank after all?' The silence that met her remark suddenly took on an ominous quality and she swung round to see Dane Goodman leaning against the door.

She caught her breath, then gulped, standing up hurriedly. 'I'm sorry, I

14

thought you were someone else . . . '
For what seemed to her an eternity he
said nothing, just stood and looked at
her with critical eyes. Half-mesmerised
she returned his stare. He was dressed
all in black this morning; needle thin
cords, and what looked like a cashmere
jersey with a round neck.

'So, you got here then . . . ' Feeling
totally intimidated by the hard look
in the brown eyes Romy just nodded.
Thick dark eyebrows suddenly snapped
together. 'Well, don't just stand there
looking like a stricken doe! I don't bite,
you know!' Horrified, she gave him a
trembling smile. 'Oh for heaven's sake!
Would you like me to play it to you?'
She moved quickly away to allow him
room, still clutching the music.

He slid onto the piano stool and
began to play the rather haunting tune
she had tentatively attempted before he
had appeared. He was giving her time
to pull herself together. Instinctively
she tried to hold herself straighter.
There were some terrifyingly high notes

to overcome and she was glad that she had spent time loosening up her voice before she arrived at the theatre.

'Well?' The last notes had died away, and Dane Goodman turned to look at her. 'Are you ready to attempt the score, or do you want to sing something you already know?'

There had been a wealth of meaning behind the words 'attempt the score'. He was trying to bully her already, and she wasn't going to accept that lying down. She raised her eyebrows. 'That's what I am here for, isn't it?' she enquired, 'so, if you're ready . . . '

Just for a moment she could have sworn there was a look of amusement on his face, but the expression had been so fleeting she thought she must have been mistaken as he launched into the opening bars saying, 'Look at me as you sing, please . . . ' His brown eyes held her slightly stormy ones until she broke the contact, ostensibly to look down at the music. She faltered slightly only once, then her strong young voice began to soar higher and higher and she forgot everything except her exhilaration in doing what she had been born for. She came back down to earth to the sounds of clapping, and turned to see that Paul Saint and his assistant, Chips, had come into the room.

She blushed faintly, and risked a quick look at the man at the piano, but he had his head down making some notes on a small pad. Suddenly all the wonderful feeling she had had while singing departed, leaving her tired and flat.

'Miss Brooke, that was glorious!' Paul Saint came up to shake her hand, a relieved smile nearly splitting his pleasant face in two. 'Where did you learn to sing?'

His enthusiasm helped her shattered confidence. 'My mother taught me until she died,' she answered shyly.

'I should say she did a remarkably good job! Was she a singer herself?'

Romy shook her head. 'Not really.

She could sing, but not well enough for a professional career so she became a teacher.'

'It's a shame she couldn't have heard you just now, I'm sure she would have been very proud!'

Romy bit her lip and looked sideways at the silent man still sitting at the piano. His decision was the important one, and so far he had said nothing. Chips handed her her coffee. Her hand shook slightly as she raised the cup to her mouth.

'You have a good natural voice, Miss Brooke, but you will need more training if you are to hold down the lead role on stage.' Dark brown eyes once more held her own. 'If you are prepared to put yourself unreservedly into my hands for the next three months and work flat out in that time, then I think I can promise you the lead role in 'Queen of the Night'.'

Romy's eyes glowed suddenly with light as she heard his words, then they dimmed as she looked down at the floor. 'Now what's the problem? Is it your boyfriend?'

Shocked, she looked up at that. 'It isn't that! It's just that I don't have enough money to live on for three months without working!'

'Is that all?' He sounded impossibly bored. 'If you work for me you'll get paid, as does everyone else in my employ.'

'But, if you think I'm not up to the part . . . I mean, why pay me if I've got to be trained?'

'God give me strength!' Dane raised his eyes to heaven before getting up from the piano and coming to stand menacingly in front of her. He put a finger under her chin and forced her to meet his eyes. 'I want a simple 'yes' or 'no' to my questions.' Temper made her own eyes darken under the implied threat. 'Do you want the starring role in my next musical?'

She gritted her teeth. 'Yes!'

'Then you'd better learn to do as I say!' He saw her mutinous expression.

'You see, it's very simple. You do what I tell you and you'll get the part, but I warn you now that I'm a professional in this game and I won't tolerate having my time wasted! I'll arrange everything for you at this end, somewhere for you to stay, your lessons, but in return I shall expect total obedience! There'll be no time in your life for outside interests, so think carefully; it's going to mean working harder than you ever have in your life.'

Romy's eyes fell under the sudden fire in his, and all the fight went out of her. She had no choice; no-one in their senses turned down an opportunity like this as no doubt he knew only too well. 'All right, I'll do what you want.'

'Good girl!' His expression softened. 'Now, how soon can you get up to London? We're going to need all the time we can get!'

Paul intervened. 'No problem, Dane! I spoke to her agent, and he's already replaced her with a girl who'd be happy to stay on if necessary.'

20

'Okay, well that's it, then. You've got the rest of this week to tidy up your life and move to London. My secretary will be in touch with you about all the details . . . ' He gave her a sudden blinding smile that showed his white teeth. 'I think you'll make a good 'Queen of the Night' Miss Brooke! Let's hope that it's the start of great things for you . . . '

Chips looked almost as bemused as she did. 'Does he always conduct auditions like that?' she asked.

He shook his head, then smiled at her. 'Quite frankly I've never seen anything like it! I mean you only sang that once didn't you?' She nodded. 'Well, there you are then. He must have been pretty sure of you to let it go at that . . . ' He gave her a sudden keen look. 'And from what I heard of your voice, I suppose I'm not really surprised. You really can hit those high notes, can't you?'

She shrugged. 'Me and a thousand others!'

'Oh no, Romy! It hasn't been that simple to find someone capable of playing Queen of the Night. Dane and Paul have been scouring the country for weeks.'

'It didn't seem to me that he was all that sure I was the right person . . . '

'He was sure all right, that's why he came along this morning. Normally he just leaves it to Paul.'

She frowned slightly. 'Just what do you think he is going to make me do in these next weeks?'

'Work on your voice I should think. It's going to be a pretty demanding role, almost operatic . . . You haven't really done much stage work have you?'

'No I haven't!' she replied, 'It's going to be quite a step up for me, isn't it?'

'Dane wouldn't bother with you if he didn't think you had what it takes. Paul and he can sound really tough at times but they're so experienced they know exactly how far they can push.

I think you'll be quite surprised at the end of it!'

She laughed then. 'Well, I hope you're right!'

Before she left the theatre Chips gave her one of the house tickets for that evening's performance. 'It's all part of the training, Romy! You can learn quite a lot about what will be expected of you just by watching Tara Tynan's performance tonight!'

# 2

Dane Goodman meant every word he had said to Romy that morning. Scotty, his super-efficient secretary, took complete charge of her life. She hardly even had time to go back north, say 'goodbye' to the girls and collect the rest of her clothes before Scotty was on the phone to her.

'Romy? I've found you a temporary room for three months in a flat in Clapham, shared with three other girls. You'll have your own room, but it's small I'm afraid. Anyway the rent is good, only thirty pounds a week, all in . . . The important thing is that you can move in this weekend. I'll have a schedule sent round of all the classes Dane wants you to attend.'

'Classes?' Romy queried.

'Yes,' Scotty answered briskly. 'I've ordered your day into a strict routine.

Dance classes in the studios at Covent Garden followed by singing classes with Dane or Betty Merriman if he's not available. There's an actor's workshop three afternoons a week which Dane wants you to join, and the other spare afternoons he wants you to learn about stage make-up and how to make the best of yourself behind the footlights!'

'Heavens! He doesn't believe in wasting time, does he?'

Scotty laughed. 'You'll soon get used to it my dear!'

She barely got past first-name terms with the other girls who were living in the flat. By the evening she was normally so tired in those first weeks that she used to disappear into her room, grateful to be alone. Inevitably she began to feel resentment towards Dane Goodman, although her singing classes with him were the brightest part of her day.

He seemed so indifferent, almost, to her as a person, as if her voice was the only thing that interested him. It didn't help that every time she had contact with him she fell more and more under his spell. Difficult and arrogant though he was most of the time, just occasionally his guard would drop if he was pleased with her, to show her glimpses of a warm, amusing personality totally at variance with his normal behaviour. Physically, his dark looks affected her far more than she thought healthy.

Towards the end of the three months she found it hard to keep her feelings of resentment to herself. They had been working on some songs from Schumann when he suddenly rounded on her.

'For heaven's sake, Romy! What the hell's got into you just lately? I've got better things to do than waste my time with you if you're not going to work!'

Guilt and despair were mixed in her face as she met his eyes defiantly. 'I'm not a machine, Dane! Just occasionally I could do with a bit of encouragement . . . '

'Could you now!' he interjected softly, 'and what sort of encouragement were you thinking of?' His dark eyes raked her body mercilessly until she could feel her whole face begin to burn. No man had ever looked at her with such lascivious amusement before. Unable to bear it any longer, she dropped her eyes and turned away from him. 'Oh yes, my dear! I know quite well what has been going on in your mind! It isn't your singing that you've been worried about, is it?' He laughed, rather unkindly. 'Grow up, Romy! You're too old for these teenage crushes. Now, pull yourself together and sing that last passage again, as it should be sung!'

Totally disconcerted by the way he had been able to read her mind, she had tried to ignore the complex mixtures of feelings he had managed to evoke in her. He made no other mention of the little episode that had just passed, as if it had been of such little importance to him that it was easily forgotten. But she had found it far harder to put out of her mind.

She knew she had learned more than she would have believed possible when she first started rushing from class to class. She certainly had more confidence in herself and in her ability to hold down a starring role. It was only with Dane himself that she still felt uncertain. For instance he never asked her to work on anything from the score of 'Queen', and apart from her one experience at her audition she was still totally in the dark about the whole project. Lately she had become more and more curious why he told her nothing about her future role. He was working her voice rather as her mother had once done, and she couldn't help wondering what he had in store for her. He had an enormous knowledge of classical music and how it should be performed. Composer of musicals he might be, but his work was based on a love of music of a very different kind.

He was a sophisticated man-of-the-world, used to the theatre, and in the public eye, whereas she was a nobody. Surprisingly she still knew nothing about his private life; whether he was married or single.

Her reserve made it difficult for her to make friends easily, anyway there was no time to relax sufficiently to make friends other than in the most superficial way.

She was resting after a particularly strenuous session in the dance studios a couple of weeks later when Scotty, rang through to her.

'Romy? Mr Goodman's had a change of plan this morning. Can you come to his house instead of the theatre?'

'Yes, I can, of course; where is it?'

Scotty gave her precise directions. 'You'd better take a taxi. Mr Goodman wants you here as soon as you can make it. I'll reimburse you when you arrive.'

So, he wanted her there in a hurry, did he? He must know, none better, that she would be tired and looking forward to the half-hour coffee break she normally allowed herself. Suddenly all the pressure that she had allowed herself to live under for the last three months fuelled her pent-up resentment until she was filled with a boiling indignation. She was tired, tired, tired and fed up with being treated like this, as if she was a child who had to do what she was told. It was about time that Dane Goodman was told where he got off as far as she was concerned.

Without waiting to change or shower, she pulled her track suit over her leotard, and grabbing her bag with her clothes went out to hail a taxi. Not even the imposing facade of the large house, facing the embankment in Chelsea, had the power to stop her. She left the taxi in a flaming temper, telling the driver to wait. Scotty opened the door, her eyebrows faintly raised as she looked at Romy.

'You were quick,' she told her, approvingly, 'although I'd have thought . . .'

Romy cut her off short. 'Where is he?' she demanded.

The eyebrows were raised a fraction. 'Up the stairs and the first door on the left, but . . . '

Romy took the stairs two at a time. She wrenched open the double doors, barely taking in the beautiful proportions of the room, just heading for the piano and the man who was sitting behind it playing softly to himself. He stood up, a faintly startled expression on his face as she moved towards him.

'Romy? You were quick, I didn't expect you quite so soon . . . '

'Didn't you?' she queried, 'I quite thought you had the impression that when you called I would come running!' His eyes narrowed as he looked at her, taking in the storm signals.

She took a deep breath. 'I've had enough of being ordered around like a child. I've run round London to all these classes without complaining, but this is it! I've had enough of you telling me what to do and when to do it. I'm quitting! Now!' Furious, she met his eyes, but he gave nothing away, just looked at her with his eyes slightly hooded. Stung at their cold appraisal, her own filled with tears. 'Can't you see?' she appealed to him furiously. 'I'm a human being in my own right, not just a voice! No-one can work well like this. I've tried and done my best but I won't do it any more; you treat me as if I'm a machine, as if I've no feelings . . . '

'I warned you, right at the start . . .'

'Yes, you did, didn't you?' She looked back at him fiercely. 'I suppose I have to thank you, you've taught me quite a lot about myself these last months. I've learnt that I can't live happily in a vacuum, that I need other people, far more than I would ever have guessed before you found me.'

'If you walk out on me now, there will be no Queen of the Night!' he told her. Astonished, she turned to face him. He came over and took her arm. 'Come and sit down. I'll order some coffee to be sent up; you look as if you need it!' She allowed him to lead her towards the enormous leather sofa in the big bay window overlooking the river. There was amusement in his face.

'Now it's my turn to tell you exactly what I've discovered about you!' Mesmerised, she allowed his suddenly warm brown eyes to hold hers. 'You have one of the most beautiful voices I have ever heard, and I knew that right from the start when I heard you in that god-awful club. You also, almost more importantly, have that ability to sing to an audience with all your heart. Call it charisma, or what you will, but nobody listening to your singing will ever be indifferent to you. That gift of yours, to establish a rapport with an audience, will make sure that you will be a star of the first magnitude. In a way, Queen of the Night was written for you, even if you only existed in my dreams then!' He bent forward then and gently kissed her lips. 'You see, Romy, although I might have a funny way of showing it, I cared enough to make sure that when you started rehearsals for the part you weren't going to feel a totally inadequate amateur among a group of professionals! Because that's what would have happened to you if we'd thrown you in at the deep end without the benefit of these months of hard work on your part.'

Totally bemused, Romy searched the brown face that was so near hers, but she saw nothing in it but laughter. 'Ah! Here's the coffee.' He got up swiftly to take the tray from Scotty. 'Hold all calls for the next hour will you?' he told his secretary. 'I don't want to be disturbed by anybody, however important it is.' He poured Romy a coffee, liberally lacing it with cream and sugar. 'Drink this, it should do you good! Also you'd better eat some of those biscuits . . . ' His eyes flickered over her figure. 'You've been losing too much weight lately which must mean that I've been working you too hard!' His eyes teased her, as if daring her to agree with him.

He waited until she had finished her coffee before speaking again. 'I was going to tell you this morning that you can drop all those classes now, because I think you are ready to start rehearsing in earnest for 'Queen of the Night'.'

A spirit of perversity made her answer. 'I'm so tired, Dane, and I'm still not quite sure if I'm up to it . . . '

His brows met in a furious frown. Romy's heart began to beat uncomfortably fast; she had been playing with fire ever since she had come to his home. The enormity of what she had just said threatened to choke her.

'Playing hard to get?' His voice sounded cold and rasping, 'Or are you still trying to pay me back for not making a pass at you?'

All the warmth had gone from his

face, leaving a cold implacable stranger. 'My God, you've got a nerve! I bring you to London, a little nobody from nowhere with everything to learn, and this is the way you repay me! You waltz in here moaning that you can't take it any more — Well, let me tell you that life at the top is damned hard, and that you don't get there without a hell of a lot of hard work and guts! There's no short cut, and if you're going to want your hand held then forget it!' He moved suddenly and took her chin in his hand. 'You can save your temperaments for the time when you've actually made it as a star, not before, do you understand?'

She nodded dumbly. 'I'm sorry, Dane. You know I'll take the role, it's just that I really am awfully tired . . . I shouldn't have said any of the things I did, and I apologise . . . ' she finished miserably.

His eyes narrowed as he studied her face carefully. 'I suppose I'd better let you have a few days off. Will you go back to your family?'

'I haven't got any family, they died just over a year ago . . . '

His hands had moved onto her shoulders, and she felt them suddenly tighten. 'You have no-one?'

'No . . . ' She stood straighter and tried to move away from him. 'I'll be fine at the flat . . . '

He swore softly under his breath. 'That's no good! Haven't you got any friends you can go and stay with?' She shook her head as he stood looking at her frowningly. 'Have you got a passport?'

Still bewildered, she tried to pull herself together. 'Yes, I have.'

'Good! Then you'd better come down to Grâcedieu with me. I was intending to fly down this evening anyway. It will do you good to get a bit of sun.'

'Grâcedieu?' she queried.

'Yes, my house just above Cannes. I normally go down there to work or to take a short break. Don't worry! I shan't expect you to do anything except relax.'

'But, but you don't want to take me! Anyway . . . '

He gave her a sharp look. 'Don't start making any more difficulties. You'll be quite safe!' She blushed heavily, uncomfortable at having her mind read. 'There's a couple who live in the house, so you won't be alone with just me. As I've still got some work to do on the final score of 'Queen' we probably won't even see much of each other. Scotty will get another ticket, so can you be back here by five o'clock?' She nodded. 'Well, go and throw a few things in a suitcase, and for God's sake keep your mouth shut about staying at Grâcedieu. If the press get wind of it, they'll make our life hell.'

'Is there, er, anyone who might get the wrong idea?' she queried delicately, 'if I'm known to have stayed with you?'

'No!' he replied smoothly, 'but don't let that give you any ideas! In spite of all the gossip to the contrary I don't have affairs with all my leading ladies!'

Still not quite sure of her luck, only knowing that it was better not to try and push it any more she enquired, 'How long will we be there for?'

'Ten days, but you can always come back early if you find you're bored!'

'Oh no!' she was shocked at his words. 'It sounds like absolute heaven, if you're sure you don't mind?'

Again he smiled at her. 'I think you'll be safer under my eye. At least this way I'll know you will be getting a proper rest, unless you intend to relax having a good time in the town?'

She shook her head decidedly. 'I've had enough of nightclubs to last me for a long long time if you remember?' she answered pertly.

He grinned at the memory of their first meeting. 'You ought to be grateful to me for taking you away from that extremely sordid atmosphere, but you realise that most of the action of my new production takes place in a night club?' His eyes looked wickedly amused at her horrified expression, 'You're a funny girl, Romy, you've never once asked about the story behind 'Queen'. Don't you want to know what sort of girl you will be playing?'

She flushed with mortification at his teasing. 'Of course I did!' she snapped back, 'but I didn't think it would be much use asking you!'

He laughed. 'You can read the whole thing down in France, then tell me what you think!'

Back at her flat she sorted out her few clothes, looking at them dubiously. There was no time to go shopping even though her bank account was surprisingly healthy; anyway she was still so over-whelmed by Dane's invitation that it was all she could do to pull herself together enough to be ready to return to his house on time.

Scotty greeted her with an expression on her face that Romy didn't altogether understand. She began to apologise.

'I'm sorry I was so foul to you, it was just that I was tired, and, well, Dane's instructions were the last straw!'

'Don't worry! I'm not surprised you suddenly blew your top! You've stood the pace remarkably well, considering,' Scotty gave her a warm smile. 'You've got to make your own way to Heathrow, for reasons I don't have to spell out I hope?'

Romy nodded. 'Yes, I understand.'

'Good! Well here are your tickets.' She handed over a smart travel folder. 'Have a good time, Romy, you deserve the rest!'

She warmed to Scotty's sudden friendliness. 'Thanks I will! I can't wait to get out to the sun . . . '

She wasn't too surprised to find that she was to be travelling tourist class, while Dane was in the first class section. It made sense for them to appear as if there was no connection between them. Dane Goodman was news, and if they were seen together, inevitably there would be comment.

41

There was even a separate car to meet her at Nice Airport. It had been a crazy day, and as she sank back comfortably into the seat she closed her eyes, unable to appreciate the unaccustomed warmth of the strangeness of everything around her.

It was Dane who woke her, shaking her shoulder. 'Wake up, sleepyhead! You're home . . . ' She opened her eyes and blinked at him, unaware of where she was. 'My God! You really are still dead to the world, aren't you?' He gave her another impatient little shake. 'Wake up, Romy! I'm not going to carry you to your room!'

His words made her pull herself together. Smothering a yawn she tried to collect her thoughts and her belongings. 'I'm sorry, Dane! I didn't mean to fall asleep . . . '

He gave her a quick look. 'There's no need to apologise!' His eyes raked her as she stood beside him, swaying slightly still from tiredness.

'You really are done in, aren't you?

I suggest you go and catch up on sleep. You'll feel better in the morning . . . '

He led her into a large airy room, filled with what seemed to be an enormous double bed.

'Sleep well, Romy! I'll see you tomorrow . . . ' Without bothering to unpack, she pulled off her clothes, and crept between smooth cool sheets that smelt faintly of lavender.

She woke slowly and stretched with a sense of well-being, her eyes slowly taking in the strange shadowy outlines of her room. Suddenly excited, she sat up and reached for her watch. She was in Dane's house in France, and already it was after eleven o'clock. She had more than slept the clock around. She got out of bed and reached for her case to find her old cotton dressing-gown.

When she walked through the big sliding windows onto the terrace outside her room she couldn't help exclaiming in delight. Grâcedieu was in the thickly wooded hills above Cannes, and her room faced towards the distant town and the sea. The thick parasol pines gave a measure of privacy from the other villas nearby. She could see their roof tiles, pink and faded in the strong sunlight. Immediately below her was an enormous swimming-pool with a number of sun loungers around it. Huge great terracotta pots were filled with bright flowers. The garden fell away beneath her in a series of terraces and she leaned out over the balcony. A disembodied voice said:

'So you're awake at last! Come on down and join me and Tina will bring you out breakfast.' As she became accustomed to the bright glare she saw tables and chairs beneath the green leaves of a vine and the shadowy form of Dane. She hurried to join him. The beauty of her surroundings made her forget to be shy with him as she tried to tell him how lovely she found everything. Not even the sight of his already sun-brown body covered with only tight fitting swimming trunks had the power to disconcert her this morning; she was bubbling with happiness and questions.

'How can you bear to be so much in London if you own this lovely house?' she asked as they were interrupted by a thickset young woman carrying a tray with a basket of warm croissants and a steaming pot of coffee which she put down carefully on the table in front of Romy.

'This is Tina,' Dane told her. 'She speaks a little English and a little French, but unless you speak Spanish, I'm afraid you will find conversation difficult!' Tina immediately broke into explosive speech which Dane answered easily. Neither of them expected Romy to join in, and the expression of ludicrous surprise on Dane's face made her want to laugh as she thanked Tina for bringing out her breakfast.

'Where did you learn to speak Spanish?' Dane asked.

'My father taught me . . . '

'Tell me about your family!' he commanded.

She shrugged her shoulders. 'There's little to tell really . . . My father taught classics at a local boys' school . . . '

'You're a girl full of surprises . . . Is there no theatrical connection in your family at all?'

She stiffened, and there was a small pause before she answered, 'Not as far as I know, unless that is you count my mother's ability to play and sing.'

'Would she have liked a theatrical career?'

'Hardly!' she answered, then took a bite of deliciously warm croissant. 'She was really only interested in classical music.'

'What would she think of you taking the lead in one of my musicals, then?' he demanded.

'She wouldn't have minded, I think, although she really wanted me to train seriously for an operatic career.'

'Would you have liked to do that?' he asked.

'I suppose, if she had still been alive, that's what I would be doing now, but as there was no money when they died, I had to go out and earn my living. Anyway I don't think my voice would have been good enough to take me to the top.'

Dane was silent for a moment, studying her intently.

'What if I told you that in my opinion your voice is good enough?'

She allowed her eyes to meet his. 'That's an academic question now, isn't it? All I want is a chance in 'Queen' to make my name.' He watched her hands clench themselves into fists.

'Is it important to you to succeed?' he asked idly.

Her eyes burned with an inner fire. 'I want it more than anything else in the world!' she answered passionately. 'I'm going to get to the top of my profession, and I don't care how long it takes!'

She missed seeing the gleam of satisfaction in his slightly heavy-lidded eyes. 'Why?' he asked.

'Why?' she queried, her beautiful

eyes still alight, 'I've just told you why!'

'No you haven't!' he answered smoothly. 'I want to know the reasons behind your ambition!'

It seemed to him that she recoiled, almost as if he had hit her. Her face had become a mask. 'My reasons are private and very personal.' A theatrical sense of timing made her hesitate, before continuing: 'But you needn't doubt me any more. I lost my temper with you yesterday because I was overtired and Scotty's call was the last straw. You've pushed me pretty hard these last three months, but underneath I've always been grateful. I won't let you down.'

When he did speak, it was almost as if he was talking to himself.

'I wonder if I'm doing the right thing, letting you take this part.' The sudden look of terror on her face made him pull himself together. 'Don't look so horrified! My misgivings are for your sake, not mine!'

'What do you mean?'

He gave her a faintly sarcastic smile. ' 'Queen of the Night' is going to be the best thing I've done so far. I'm also pretty certain that it's going to put you right at the top! Are you going to be able to handle that?'

'Of course I am!'

'You're very young, aren't you? It isn't always a good thing to have one's dream come true too quickly . . . '

'You are always going on about my age!' she answered resentfully. 'I'm not likely to lose my head if that's what you're afraid of! Anyway, just taking the leading role in one show isn't enough to build up the sort of reputation I want.'

An unwilling laugh broke from him. 'My God! You've got it all worked out, haven't you? And I suppose I'm just a stepping stone on the way! There I was thinking we'd have to take everything slowly because you were shy and more than a little insecure . . . ' He shook his head in disbelief. 'How wrong can you be?'

'No! I mean you were right!' she protested. 'I wasn't sure, and I'm still not because you haven't let me see the part!'

'Ah! So that's been worrying you, has it? Well . . . ' He turned and brought out a thick folder. 'When I think you've had enough of a rest I'll let you read the libretto first then later on I'll play you the score.'

He added, 'I shall be out for the rest of the day, but we'll meet for dinner.' He moved forward out into the sunlight, then ran and dived smoothly into the big pool.

# 3

Romy sat alone after Dane had left. He had no idea of the forces that drove her and she hoped he never would. They were all part of the past and she intended them to stay there. Dane had disconcerted her by sensing there were things she would rather not talk about but for all her ambition, she hadn't been pretending since she had met him.

She did feel shy and insecure in his company. He knew so much about the world she hoped to enter that doubts about her own ability had inevitably made her feel inadequate. All she had to sustain her was her ambition and the determination to prove to . . . Furious with the path her thoughts had taken she wrenched them away from the familiar bitter trail and walked out into the bright sunlight. She settled herself down onto one of the sun loungers.

Later she retreated thankfully into the shade of the vine, grateful for George's offer to drive her into Cannes. Her thoughts had given her no rest; she needed to stimulate herself with outside interests. Also she was all too conscious of Dane's absence, so it would be fun to go on a shopping spree.

Tina wasn't the slightest bit offended that Romy should decide to eat in town. In fact she went to considerable trouble to tell her where she could find cheap, pretty clothes. 'You don't need to go to the big shops to find nice things. There is a market where we go to buy the vegetables,' she told Romy, 'and they sell clothes in another square quite close.'

Romy was grateful. 'Thanks, Tina!' she grinned, 'but George needn't wait for me. I'll take a taxi back to the villa.'

The little maid looked doubtful for a moment. 'Mr Dane, he tells us to look after you. I think it is better that George waits for you.'

'For heaven's sake, Tina!' Romy protested. 'I'm not a child, I'll be fine on my own.'

Tina's chin lifted a little. 'George won't mind, and Mr Dane, well, maybe he would be cross if we left you alone.' Her eyes suddenly creased with amusement. 'You're a special lady to him! He told me so!'

Later, as Romy walked around the markets in Cannes she found it difficult to concentrate entirely on what she was doing. Tina's last words and the look that went with them . . . if only she could believe that he was interested in her as a person, not just as his future star.

She was staring into the window of a small boutique. The clothes so cleverly displayed there brought her mind smartly back to the present. Dreams about Dane should be banished into the realm of make-believe where they belonged, she told herself sharply, as she pushed open the door and walked in.

Two hours later she wandered idly up the Boulevard de la Croisette, amusing herself watching the people stretched out on the expensive beaches below her. She walked confidently, her new sundress and the large shady hat protecting her face guaranteeing that she caught and held attention. Romy hadn't been able to resist the temptation to explore Cannes in one of her new outfits. Cut very short, the green dress exposed her long legs, her pale skin in stark contrast to the clothing and suntans everyone else seemed to have. She knew perfectly well that she was attracting a great deal of awareness from most of the men, and she found their sometimes vocal comments amusing and good for her morale. Her new sunglasses added an air of mystery to her face she thought, as her long legs walked easily over the broad pavement towards the place where George was to pick her up.

'Well, well, well! I thought I'd left you safely by my pool. What induced you to come into Cannes in the heat of the day?'

Romy turned quickly, drawing off her sunglasses. 'Dane!' He had to be aware of her delighted pleasure, and a rueful smile twisted his lips as he looked her over carefully. She took hold of his arm. 'I've been shopping, of course!'

'Of course!' he agreed gravely, but there was a laugh in his voice. 'An eye-catching little number, I have to agree, but don't tell me this is all you've acquired?'

'Oh no!' Her eyes were lit with happiness. 'I've left the rest with George, he's picking me up in about twenty minutes.'

'Poor George!' He fell into step with her, 'But you're an idiot to have come out in this heat; it would have been better to wait until this evening. Anyway, I'm surprised there are any shops open!'

'Oh, I came in late this morning, not long after you left.'

He frowned. 'Have you had any lunch?'

'No, but I wasn't hungry. I had a huge breakfast rather late if you remember!'

'It wouldn't hurt you to put on a few more pounds, Romy. Come on, I'll buy you something now.' She clung on to his arm, delighting in the feel of its hard muscled strength under her hand and with his companionship. She could feel that he was aware of her; his eyes slid over her in amused appreciation.

'What a child you are!' Dane teased, as he sat her down at the café where George was to meet her, and ordered an enormous concoction of fruit and ice cream. 'This ought to help restore your energy!'

She protested, 'I haven't eaten anything like that for years!'

He gave her a grin. 'Don't tell me you have to watch your figure?' Again he allowed his eyes to linger over her slender curves. 'I told you in London you had lost too much weight.'

'You can't be too rich or too thin!'

'I don't think most men would agree with you!' His eyes and voice were teasing, 'I like a few curves, always supposing they are in the right places.' This time there was no mistaking where his eyes were lingering. Romy felt suddenly breathless as she saw his eyes studying the swell of her breasts. It seemed to her that time suddenly stopped, and the air between them became electrically charged. She looked at his brown arm, covered in dark hair, that lay so close to hers. By a supreme effort of will she was able to stop herself touching him.

'M'sieu, Mam'selle?' The waiter arrived, placing the tall glass of ice-cream and fresh peaches in front of her.

'I expect you to eat it all,' Dane warned her, his mouth twitching with amusement at her slightly horrified expression.

'Couldn't you even manage a teaspoon?' she pleaded.

'Well, I might, if you think you can spare some,' he teased. He moved his head close to hers as he picked up his tiny coffee spoon and helped himself.

She giggled, trying hard not to be overcome by the subtle, faintly lemon smell of his aftershave. 'I think we'd better ask for another spoon, don't you think? You aren't going to be much help with that one.'

His eyes were warm, the gold in them glinting in the sunlight as they met hers. 'But I ordered this for you, and I want you to eat it!' She felt her whole body tighten under the melting, almost caressing tone of his voice as she picked up the long spoon and began to eat. 'Good?' he queried.

'Mmm, delicious . . . Maybe I was hungry after all!'

There was satisfaction in his voice as he answered. 'You need someone to look after you, Romy! You're crazy to skip meals.'

'Well, I won't be able to for the next ten days, will I? You'll take care of that, as you do of everything else in my life!'

'You don't like being told what to do, do you?'

'I suppose I'm not used to it,' she answered thoughtfully. 'I've got used to thinking for myself this last year.'

'Has it been hard?'

The kindness in his voice nearly brought tears to her eyes. She forced herself to answer. 'I don't suppose it's easy for anyone to find themselves suddenly alone, but I was lucky, I managed to find work quite quickly.'

'I find it extraordinary that you have no-one that can be called family!'

Unconsciously she sat a little straighter in her chair, her hand tightening on the spoon. From his narrowed eyes she knew he was aware of her tension. 'Why?' she countered. 'Lots of people don't have much family. Anyway, what about you? Do you have lots of brothers and sisters?'

'No, I'm an only child like yourself, and although my father died a few years ago, I do have a mother, also uncles and aunts and a few cousins here and there!'

'Are any of them in the business?'

'No, none of them, except my mother's brother. He is director of music at a cathedral in the west country.'

She laughed. 'Most serious musicians look down from a great height on the things we do, don't they?'

'They do?' he queried. 'How many serious musicians do you know?'

A pit had opened up in front of her, the shock of his words made her feel faint, driving all the colour from her face. 'I — I'm sorry . . . ' She stood up quickly, frantically trying to think of something to say, anything, so he would not go on questioning her. 'I feel a bit sick . . . '

He stood up quickly, pressing her shoulders down, so she was forced to sit again. 'You little fool! You shouldn't

have come out in the heat of the day.'
He looked round quickly for a waiter.

'Don't worry, Dane! Look, here's
George, he can take me home.'

There was a worried expression in
his eyes, but she had regained some
of her colour.

'Truly, Dane, I'm all right now!
I expect it was the heat, and my
tummy's not really used to eating rich
foods . . . '

'If you say so?' He was aware that
that was not the whole truth.

She gave him a tremulous smile.
'You were right, I just felt a little
faint, it must be the heat.'

He helped her over to the car. 'When
you get back, go straight to bed! I'll
get Tina to bring you your dinner on
a tray.' He spoke quickly to George.

'I'm sorry, Dane, I didn't mean to
be a nuisance.'

'No, I don't suppose you did! You're
just going to have to learn to take better
care of yourself in the future, otherwise
you won't be up to taking on the lead

in 'Queen'.' His face softened, and he bent forward to kiss her lightly on the cheek, 'But you're still a little idiot!' He shut the door of the car, and George pulled away.

Romy felt frightfully guilty to start with, as both Dane and Tina treated her as if she was a fragile piece of porcelain, hardly allowing her to do anything for herself, but after a couple of days she began to rather enjoy being looked after so carefully. It was very nice to be cherished for a change, after the loneliness of the last year. Dane was at his most charming, so much so that she began to believe that perhaps she did matter to him as a person after all. Her stern music teacher became a creature of the past, his place taken by a warm, smiling man who amused her and made her laugh.

Her skin gradually turned to a pale gold, and after she had been at Grâcedieu for a week she was bursting with health and vitality. One morning at breakfast Dane carelessly tossed the score of 'Queen' into her lap.

'I think the time has now come for you to see just exactly what it is you've committed yourself to!' he teased. 'I've got to go out for the rest of the day, but this should keep you quiet . . . ' He grinned at the way her eyes had suddenly brightened. 'Of course you might not be so enthusiastic when you've read it all, but I'll play you the score after dinner tonight!' He gave her cheek a careless flick with one finger then walked away into the house.

Determinedly, she settled herself down on one of the sun loungers and began to read. Two hours later she retreated into the shade, trying to hide her excitement. Dane was right, this had to be the best thing he had ever done, and it was no longer surprising that he had worked her so hard. Already she could feel butterflies in her tummy at the thought of playing 'Giselle'. She could understand why he had told her nothing because if she had realised three months ago just exactly what the part entailed she might well have given up before she started.

It was a classic story of love gone wrong, a tragedy, and the plot centred round a young singer whose love was destroyed by a greedy man who wanted to exploit her talent for his own good. It was set in London just before the start of the last war. Giselle was a night-club singer who fell in love with a young soldier who came every night to hear her. The owner, Harry, half in love with Giselle himself and becoming rich from the way she was able to draw in the crowds, was furious when the affair began to look serious. If Giselle left to get married then he would lose everything, so he set out to destroy their love.

He found out that Edward, the man Giselle loved, was more than a little jealous of her popularity with other men. Harry deliberately fed his fears, fomenting trouble between them, until his final coup where he made it appear to Edward that she had another lover. Furiously jealous, Edward walks out on Giselle, leaving her imagining that she is not good enough for him.

Miserable and bitter at what she sees as his betrayal, she turns to Harry, who offers her warmth and sympathy. Meanwhile war has been declared and Edward has left London for France. Harry manages to persuade her to be his wife, but the night before their wedding she hears that Edward has been killed at Dunkirk.

Harry, in his clumsy efforts to comfort her inadvertently lets her find out that he played a part in separating her from Edward. She plots her revenge! she will kill herself, joining her one true love in death, leaving Harry with nothing.

On sight-reading Dane's score she found some beautiful, haunting melodies at the start which strengthened into an almost operatic role which she guessed would test her voice to the utmost. Impatient, she walked round to the music room but found the big sliding doors locked.

'Mr Dane, he guessed you would want the piano!' Tina told her slyly. 'He wants you to wait until this evening, then he will play it all to you himself.'

'But Tina, it's only just lunchtime now!' Romy wailed. 'How am I to wait that long?'

'Lunch is ready, now, so you come and eat. Mr Dane tells me if you do not eat, then he will make you wait until tomorrow to hear the score!' Romy knew Dane well enough by now to know that if she didn't eat then he would have no compunction at making her wait even longer.

She read and reread the score, but found it impossible to relax. Not even swimming concentrated lengths in the pool had the power to release her from the spell of 'Queen'. There were far too many questions that only Dane could answer.

She was ready long before he was,

sitting impatiently on the terrace under the vine, watching the sun slowly sink into the horizon. She was wearing a simple blue cotton dress, cut low in the neck, just showing the swell of her breasts. She wore high-heeled sandals in a soft blue kid that emphasised her long, elegant dancer's legs.

Dane joined her silently as she sat broodingly sipping the cold white wine which Tina had brought out, occasionally eating an olive from the bowl in front of her. She jumped, suddenly realising she was not alone.

He gave her a grin before helping himself to a glass of wine. 'Your nerves must be in a bad way to make you react like that.'

She gave him a resentful look. 'There's nothing wrong with my nerves!'

He laughed. 'I'm glad to hear it, I thought you might be worried after reading 'Queen'.'

'Well, let's just say that I can understand why you wouldn't let me see it before!' she answered tartly, before turning a glowing face to his. 'I think it is fantastic, although I find it hard to believe you really think I'm up to the part?'

He saw the worry in her eyes. 'I do. I always did, right from the first moment I heard you!'

Her smile was slightly strained. 'You're sure that wasn't because I was singing in a nightclub?'

'Don't be silly!' His voice was matter-of-fact. 'If I didn't think you could do it, then why should I have wasted so much time on you these last three months?'

She gave a helpless shrug of her shoulders. 'If you say so, then I suppose it's got to be all right!' She smiled, 'It's certainly a peach of a part, and from what I could read of the score it's got some fantastic music to go with it! Who wrote the play?'

'Luke Seaward. I hope this will be the start of a new partnership. We've got a couple of other ideas simmering away in the pot, and if this is the success we all hope, well, who knows? He wants to meet you.'

'And I'd very much like to meet him,' she agreed enthusiastically. 'Have you thought who will be playing Edward and Harry?'

He named two actors very well known in the English theatre. 'Simon Canter will play Edward and Mark Haslam, Harry.'

'Wow!'

He saw the awe in her face. 'Don't let them intimidate you! They both know very well that the success of 'Queen' depends upon who plays 'Giselle'. Now, let's eat, then I'll play you the whole score.'

Romy would never forget the evening that followed. Dane played the score right the way through, and by the end she had tears in her eyes. The big sliding doors of the music room were open and moonlight poured in over the polished wooden floor. Dane played with a light behind him that threw dramatic shadows onto his expressive face as she lay stretched out on the large sofa, watching every play of emotion on his face, remembering Luke Seaward's words as the music brought them to life. The last theme was so poignantly sad that tears fell silently down her cheeks.

'Hey!' He came to sit next to her, putting one arm around her as she turned her head into his shoulder. 'What an emotional little thing you are!' His voice sounded deep and soothing. He handed her a clean, white handkerchief. 'I hope the tears are a compliment!' Slowly she came back to reality, 'Well?' he demanded.

'Oh, Dane!' She gave him a watery smile. 'It's the most beautiful thing I've ever heard!'

'Good!' She heard the satisfaction in his voice. 'Now put it right out of your mind. The day will come, all too soon I fear, when you'll be sick to death of it!'

'Never!' she protested vehemently.

He laughed. 'Well, I hope it won't

bore you too quickly. We plan to take it to Broadway after the London run. God knows who we are going to find to understudy you. I hope you're tougher than you look . . . We'll start work on the score when we get back to London. I want two or three songs pre-released before we start on the production. Paul Saint will be in charge then, so you won't be seeing so much of me in the future. But for the moment, Romy, I want you to take every advantage of your holiday out here. When we get home then the real work will start!'

'You've been so kind to me,' she told him softly, 'I hope I can repay you by being a success as 'Giselle'.'

'That's a very charitable view of my motives, I could just be looking after my investment!'

She slid away from him, then asked, 'And are you?'

'No, you minx!' He pulled her back against him, his eyes once more narrowed with silent laughter as he looked down into her face. He took her chin into his hand, his expression suddenly serious. 'You intrigue me, you know! You're such an extraordinary mixture of naïvety and ruthlessness. I wish I could be sure that your crush on me isn't just because you think I can help your career!'

He watched the hurt in the wide eyes, and almost as if he couldn't help himself he bent forward and allowed his lips to meet hers. Romy felt as if her bones had turned to water as with one fluid movement she melted against his lean strength. Her lips trembled slightly under his, then parted under his urgent demand so she could taste the sweetness of his tongue lightly exploring her mouth. The kiss deepened, and one of his hands gently cupped one breast. He pushed her back on the sofa, his weight pressing her body deep into the soft cushions. She quivered under the unfamiliar sensations that were flooding through her, but made no protest as his hands first found, then undid the row of buttons down the front of her dress, exposing her breasts in their flimsy black lace covering. She felt the sudden hard surge of his masculinity, his whole body tightening with excitement as his eyes tried to pierce what was so casually hidden from him. His hands slid behind her back until his fingers found, then released the catch of her bra.

He gave a long sigh of pleasure as he pushed the offending material away, his thumbs gently brushing over the evidence of her arousal. He bent his head and allowed his mouth to close over one rosy nipple, and she gave a sigh of pleasure, her hands restlessly moving through his thick dark hair.

The movement of his tongue was driving her mad as he explored her breasts, her mouth, tracing a path of fire over her sensitised skin. Her flesh looked impossibly white next to the gypsy darkness of his as she dragged off his shirt to pull the smoothly muscled chest down to her, his mouth once more teasing and tantalising hers until she was in a state of mindless abandon.

She could feel his mounting excitement and it drove her to a further pitch of erotic abandon. She wriggled out of her remaining clothes, her heated body longing for the relief that only he could give her.

'Christ, Romy . . . ' his voice sounded thick and slurred, 'do you always come on as strong as this?'

It took a moment for his words to penetrate the red mist of her desire, then she half turned away from him, burying her face in one of the sofa cushions. Her voice sounded muffled. 'I don't know . . . This has never happened to me before . . . '

'What?' He half sat up and looked down at her, and unable to help herself she put up a finger to trace the contours of his mouth, sensual lips that had just given her so much pleasure. 'Romy!' he half-groaned her name, 'What do you mean, this hasn't happened before?'

Once more she hid her face from him. 'It's just that . . . well . . . there's never been another man . . . '

He swore softly. 'Do you mean you're still a virgin?'

She nodded her head, doubts about her previous behaviour making her whole body burn with a sudden, violent flush. The atmosphere had subtly altered, and she was ashamed of her nakedness. He stood up, moving away from the sofa, and she hurriedly pulled on her clothes. He had moved towards the big windows, his body now bathed in the cool silver light of the moon, his silhouette dark and somehow menacing.

She was suddenly afraid of what he might say. 'We'll forget what has just happened, won't we?' Her voice, unnaturally high, rushed on. 'I don't know what happened to me, I don't usually behave like that . . . It must be the moonlight and your music . . . ' She could see the stunned expression on his face, and she tried to slip past him out of the door.

'No! Romy, wait . . . You can't just walk out and pretend nothing has happened!'

'Why not? Nothing important has happened has it? It was only a kiss, and I'm sure you've kissed hundreds of women, so why worry?' She ran out into the moonlight, desperate to escape the most humiliating experience that had ever happened to her.

# 4

Alone in her room, she locked the door and drew the curtains. Dane hadn't followed her so he must be disgusted by her wanton behaviour, just as she was ashamed of herself. Why, why had she allowed herself to be so carried away? He was the most exciting and fascinating man she had ever met, but that didn't excuse her brazen behaviour.

Was she in love with him? She didn't know, she just knew that lying in his arms had been heaven. After all she still knew very little about him, except that he was rich and powerful and no man with his looks could be unaware of the effect they had on the opposite sex. He had implied that there was no-one special in his life, but that didn't necessarily mean he lived like a monk.

She sat up on the bed, certain of one thing; nothing must be allowed to jeopardise her role in 'Queen'. However much she might regret her behaviour tonight she would meet him for breakfast tomorrow morning and behave as if nothing had happened between them. He would guess it was an act but it would give him an easy way out, and that had to be what he wanted.

After a restless night she was up early and had a glorious swim which helped to release some of her tension but by no means all of it. Their coming meeting was going to test her powers as an actress to the utmost, but he must never be allowed to guess how deeply humiliated she felt.

Dane joined her at the breakfast table, and a quick glance at his face made her heart sink. He looked as if he had had a bad night, and hadn't bothered to shave. There was a wary expression on his face as he looked at her.

'Hi!' she greeted him brightly, 'I've just had the most heavenly swim. I must say if this house was mine I don't think I'd ever want to leave!'

His mouth suddenly set into grim lines as he answered, 'So that's the way you intend to play it!'

Romy crossed her fingers, hidden in her lap, and allowed a smile to just twist the ends of her mouth. 'What other way is there?' she asked simply.

He shrugged his shoulders in a faintly irritable way. 'Why did you run away last night?' His eyes, dark and intent, fastened on her face.

She twisted her hands nervously. This was worse than she expected. 'I, well, I . . . Oh hell! You know damn well why I left! Look, please can't we just forget it?'

'It meant so little to you that you'd prefer to pretend that it didn't happen?'

'I, well . . . Isn't that the best way?' she appealed to him, trying to ignore the heavy frown that had suddenly blackened his face.

He looked suddenly very tired as well as cross.

'All right, all right, forget it, if that's what you want! But let me warn you my dear, if you play with fire, one day you're likely to get burnt!' He looked up into her slightly horrified face. 'Do you want to cut this break short and go home?'

Her shattered surprise was written all too clearly on her face. 'If you think it would be better . . . ' she muttered, her face averted.

'No! No of course I don't think it would be better,' he suddenly shouted at her, 'I just wondered if you'd rather leave after what happened between us. Good God! Do I have to spell everything out to you?'

Romy felt her face going scarlet. 'If you mean do I still trust you, then the answer's yes . . . I love it here,' she told him, her voice sounding unnatural and stilted, 'that's if you're sure you don't mind me staying on?'

He gave a careless shrug of his

shoulders. 'It makes no difference to me either way what you choose to do, but I think you'd be better staying on here in the sun.'

His attraction for her this morning was even more potent than last night, the rough sensuality of his presence almost overpowering.

'Don't worry, Romy! I've decided that it isn't a good idea for us both to be alone here together. I've got some guests arriving today so you'll be able to relax!' He sounded sarcastic and faintly bored, and she knew that whatever had happened between them was over and finished. 'Tina and George could probably do with a hand this morning to help with all the extra shopping,' he continued.

She tried hard to hide the sudden brilliance in her eyes as she turned her head away to avoid the slightly cruel look on his face. The caring kindness which had surrounded her was also to be a thing of the past. 'Of course,' she answered quietly, 'I'd be happy to help.' She found her dark glasses in her bag, and put them on, then stood up and left the table, her humiliation now total and complete.

There was no denying that the whole sorry mess had been made by her in the first place. At least she would still be near him, even though it looked as if that was going to be cold comfort.

When she returned with George and Tina from the shopping trip it was to find the villa already full of people, and for the rest of her time there he tried to ensure they were never alone. It seemed that Dane had turned Grâcedieu into an open house because new people came and went all the time.

Dane introduced her carelessly as his latest star, but his manner made it all too clear that their relationship was only a professional one on his part.

She flirted outrageously with anyone who gave her the opportunity, but she felt angry and forlorn inside when she saw him behaving in exactly the same way.

Why didn't he realise, she thought resentfully that she had only been trying to defuse a potentially explosive situation. She suffered agonies of jealousy when she saw his lazy, knowing smile at one young actress who was wearing only the most minimal of monokinis. She refused to analyse her emotions, preferring to salvage her pride by allowing Dean Masters, the talented young American actor, to monopolise her attention. More than once she was conscious of Dane's eyes on her.

As the days rolled by it became clearer and clearer that Dane's brooding presence still had far too much power for her to forget him for a single second.

Just occasionally, as she found his eyes fixed on her, she fancied that his interest in her was as strong as ever, but she concentrated on extracting every ounce of pleasure she could from this strange bitter-sweet break.

However, she found she couldn't continue to be in Dane's company without it causing her acute pain, so she found excuses to be by herself more and more. As she explored the lower terraces of his garden she found peace of a sort by being alone.

One particularly still and beautiful evening she had excused herself early from dinner and wandered to one of the lower terraces. A nightingale was singing and she allowed her voice to blend and mingle with it, striving for the same sweet purity of sound. She was disconcerted, then amazed, when the nightingale answered her back, as if trying to outsing this strange intruder. She didn't notice that she was no longer alone until the bird fell mysteriously silent.

She swung round to find someone standing behind her although it was too dark by then to see who it was. But as she was held close to long, lean strength, her own body had no doubts as to who held her so tightly. Her lips opened under the firm demanding pressure of Dane's mouth. Languorous pleasure, mixed with sweet pain had her responding with joyous abandon as his hold on her tightened. Neither spoke, just drank deeply of the sensual enchantment each gave to the other, so close, that time ceased to have any meaning.

A plaintive voice, crying 'Dane, Dane' seemed to be just an echo of her own heart, but the man in her arms suddenly stiffened, then thrust her rudely away from him. Half stumbling, she fell against a narrow bench, and allowed her body to slump against the still-warm stone, trying desperately to come to terms with the fact that nothing had really changed between them.

On her last day she found him alone in the big drawing-room. On the surface she glowed with health and a new-found beauty, but underneath she felt disturbed and unhappy. She thanked him for her holiday.

'I'm glad you've had a good time, Romy. Given enough men to flirt with, you blossom?'

Stung, she answered sharply, 'You haven't exactly deprived yourself either, have you?'

'Jealous?' he enquired.

'I've no right to be, have I? You're just my boss, as you've made all too clear!'

He heard the bitterness in her voice, and his voice was grim as he answered, 'Yes! So you'd better not forget it, had you? There'll be no time for boyfriends once you're back in London, so you'll have to keep that abandoned little body of yours in check!'

Furious, her eyes filled with tears, and this time she was too angry to bother to wipe them away. 'You'll never let me forget, will you? Why can't you accept that it was partly your fault? You even tried it again in the garden that night, didn't you? Until of course — ' here her voice dripped with sarcasm, 'you decided that enough was enough and you'd better go and look after your other guests! You make me sick, Dane!'

He lunged for her, his nostrils white and pinched with rage. 'I make you sick, do I? I don't think so, Romy, as I'll prove to you right this minute . . . '

She tried to fight him, but he held her hair, forcing her face to his, until his lips found hers, seeking, punishing, until helplessly she gave him the response he had been waiting for. At once his hold on her loosened, softened, and his tongue gently licked away the tears still silently falling from her closed eyes. 'No . . . ' she breathed, fighting to regain control.

'Yes, Romy!' he whispered, 'Why deny what you feel?'

'No!' She wrenched herself out of his arms, 'Please, Dane, I don't want any of this!'

'Don't be so dramatic! That was just to keep you in line. If you're going to succeed as 'Giselle' then you're going to have to learn to keep your emotions under control for the next few months!'

The mention of 'Giselle' helped to steady her. He had thrown her off balance, just as he always would as soon as he held her in his arms. It meant nothing to him, she knew that now; she had better leave while she still had a little dignity left.

Alone in her room she couldn't help wondering if he found anything special in her kisses, then chided herself for her foolishness. Dane was out of her class, and the sooner she accepted that the happier she would be. She must concentrate single-mindedly on her career because that was the only thing that was important.

On the day after her return to London, Romy called round to Dane's Chelsea house. Scotty greeted her with a curious look. 'Well? How did it go, Romy? You certainly look a different girl!'

'Oh great! I had a wonderful time,' she answered with enforced heartiness.

'And Dane? How is he? I thought you might have returned together?'

Romy couldn't help blushing a little. 'He's fine! I don't know when he's coming back, at the moment the villa is full of people!'

'Full of people? That's not like him at all! Usually he goes down there to rest. Are you sure?'

'Well, it certainly was yesterday before I left.'

'I wonder why?' Scotty mused, 'Usually he keeps well away from all the show business groupies down there.' Again Romy was conscious of the sharply interested stare. She picked up a sheet of paper and handed it over. 'Here's the list of your appointments for the next week, Romy. This afternoon you are due at the lawyers to meet your agent and sign the contract for the lead role in 'Queen'. Rehearsals are due to start in six weeks' time. Alistair Gethin, the conductor, is expecting to start work with you almost immediately on the score. Three numbers have been chosen for pre-release, two of them your solos, and a duet between Simon Canter and Mark Haslam.'

'At the end of the week there is to

be a meeting between you, Paul Saint, Luke Seaward and Mark and Simon.'

Romy let her breath out in a gentle sigh as she studied the neatly typed page. Her life was really going to get into top gear, but the idea didn't frighten her as it once might have done. She was going to succeed because 'Queen' couldn't be allowed to fail.

'I'm afraid you're going to have to get out of the flat in Clapham fairly soon,' Scotty told her, 'but don't worry, I think the alternative's almost been taken care of.'

Even that news didn't worry her. She no longer doubted that Scotty would find her somewhere else.

At the flat there was a message for her to call Tara Tynan. Intrigued, she called the number straight away. Tara had had the lead role in 'Greymask' and was going over to the States with the show in a couple of weeks' time. She wasted no time in coming to the point.

'I wonder if you'd be interested in

taking over the lease on my mews house?'

After her session with the lawyers this afternoon, money obviously wasn't going to be too much of a problem for Romy.

'It's not too far from the theatre,' Tara told her, 'and it's quite reasonable because the lease is due to run out in a couple of years. So all you've got to do is agree to get out then.'

Romy agreed enthusiastically to go and see it, and was charmed by what she found. Downstairs there was just the one room, with a small kitchen leading off it, and a spiral staircase to the upper floor with two double bedrooms and a bathroom.

'The word is out already that 'Queen' is going to be a smash hit, and that you're going to be London's newest star,' Tara told Romy, wrily. 'Perhaps it's a good thing I'm going to the States!'

'Would you have liked the part?' Romy asked shyly.

'No way!' the other girl responded quickly, perhaps too quickly. 'Anyway, I haven't got the voice. They say Paul is combing some of the smaller operatic companies trying to find an understudy for you!' Romy frowned for a moment.

'Surely not?'

'Yes, darling! If Dane's going to write for you in the future, then I can't see the rest of us getting much of a look-in!' She stood up quickly in a sudden, graceful movement. 'Do you want a coffee?'

Romy readily agreed. Maybe she would now find out about Dane and his life.

'By the way, do you want to buy the contents? I don't believe in cluttering myself up with possessions. If I can make it over there, I don't think I'll bother to come back!' Romy thought she heard a hint of bitterness behind the brave words and said softly, 'Hey! It's not that bad is it?'

Tara shrugged her shoulders. 'No, not really, but it's going to be quite an effort to start over! I'm the only one of the cast going; the rest of them stay here and do a tour with my understudy! It's too complicated to take them over to the States. It means I shall have to get used to a new producer . . . Oh forget it! I sound a right little bitch, don't I? But I don't mean it, I'm just a bit tired, that's all . . . It's great being up there in front of the lights, knowing most of the audience have come to see you, but it can play havoc with the rest of your life!'

Tara changed the subject. 'Dane seems to have writing musicals down to a fine art. I mean there isn't anyone else over here to touch him, is there? Still, now he has broken up with Eddie Linell for good, maybe 'Greymask' will be the last great success.' She looked at Romy's horrified face. 'Don't be a goose! I didn't mean 'Queen'. That's quite different I gather from his usual work. I suppose he's going back to his roots at last.'

'What do you mean?'

'He was at the Royal College of Music for years, wasn't he? Perhaps he'll go back to writing the sort of music that he was trained for in the first place.'

'I don't think so,' said Romy, 'at least not yet. He told me that he's got a couple more ideas that he thinks will work with Luke Seaward.'

Tara gave her a sharp look. 'He doesn't usually discuss his work until it's well advanced.'

Romy wondered if she had been indiscreet, but Tara went on:

'He's a tough bastard to work for, I warn you! He's got damn high standards and heaven help you if you fall short of them. There you are, quietly rehearsing, not dreaming he is anywhere around, when up he pops up like the demon king! 'No, no, Tara!' she mimicked. 'You've got your breath control all wrong'.'

Romy couldn't help laughing, Tara had caught exactly Dane's impatient manner.

'You might well laugh now, but just you wait till it happens to you!'

'Don't worry, I do know! He's been giving me singing lessons for the past three months.'

'Well, I wish you all the luck in the world, darling! I hope 'Queen' succeeds for Dane's sake, because he must be feeling pretty miserable now Angie's made up her mind which one of them she wants!' Romy looked a query. 'Angela Tree, of course! She's done pretty well for herself since she had the lead role in 'Whistle down the Wind'. Both Dane and Eddie were mad about her, but she didn't want to be tied down until she had really got her career off the ground. She always wanted to get into films, and it looks as if she has succeeded at long last. I gather Eddie's moving out to California to be with her . . . ' She was silent for a moment. 'Dane must be pretty cut up about it all, now he's lost her and his partner as well. She's probably done the right thing though,

95

because she isn't really interested in music, and music is Dane's life, as if you didn't know! Now let's get down to business shall we?'

It was a new experience for Romy not to have to worry too much about money, but she still thought she had got a bargain as they shook hands at last. It would mean she would have to be careful again for the next few months, but at least she now had a roof over her head.

She left the small house that would so soon be hers, with her head in a whirl, but with a heavy heart. So Dane was in love with Angela Tree was he? Angie Tree's blonde good looks were almost as well known to her as her own face. She had appeared on television over the last couple of years in a number of starring roles. Her face stared out at one from posters all over London, and she was beloved by the tabloid press.

Romy walked rather blindly along the streets. Surely the papers would have picked up what Tara had told her? Maybe the story hadn't broken yet. She tried to concentrate, to remember what she had read about Angie lately. Romy was sure there was nothing about her impending marriage to Eddie Linell. She had only seen photos of him, but compared to Dane he was nothing. It would be very easy to love Dane. All at once she felt sick. She turned, rather blindly, into a small public park and sat down on one of the benches. Why, she loved him herself.

She had loved him for months, and if she had used her head at all she should have realised long ago the danger she was in. He was in love with one of the most beautiful women in the theatre today, so it was hardly surprising that he had no time for her, apart from their professional commitment.

She was pretty enough, she supposed, but no-one had ever described her as beautiful. All she did have that interested Dane was a good voice. She didn't even know about men, and her one experience with Dane had shattered what little confidence she had.

Even if Tara's story was true, she could hardly see him turning to her for comfort. He called her a child, found her naïve, and had rejected her when she offered herself to him. She had only herself to blame for the whole, stupid mess. She must ignore the pain that threatened to choke her; she forced her mind to concentrate on something else that Tara had told her that had filled her with illogical foreboding, so much so, that for a moment she completely forgot her problems and prayed fervently that what she feared would not happen.

# 5

Romy had been rather dreading meeting her fellow actors and Luke Seaward, but it went very well, particularly after they had heard her sing. Already she had had several sessions with Alistair Gethin, the conductor, and had found him easy to work with and impressed with her voice. It was at his suggestion that she sang to them the first of her two solos.

'Well!' Simon Canter had said, after a moment of stunned silence when she had finished, followed by immediate applause. 'Now we know why Dane was so keen to make us wait for our leading lady! I can see who's going to steal all the limelight in this production!' His lively blue eyes crinkled up in his good-looking face. 'It doesn't look as if we are going to have to look for more work for quite a while, does it, Mark?' He appealed to the slightly older man who was to play Harry.

'No indeed it doesn't!' Mark replied, in his deep voice. 'I think we are all going to be in on the birth of a new star . . . Well done my dear!'

Luke Seaward turned out to be a quiet, bespectacled man, rather intense and serious at first sight, but he, too, pronounced himself more than satisfied with her as 'Giselle'. 'In fact Dane was quite right, as usual! He told me that not only could you sing the part divinely, you were also beautiful as well!'

Luke's words gave Romy a lovely warm feeling. Dane had said she was beautiful!

'Right!' Paul raised his voice. 'You've all got five weeks to get familiar with your parts. We'll be rehearsing in the Methodist Hall in Brixton as usual until we're ready for the theatre. Rafe Dubois is going to be doing the scenery, and we've been lucky enough to get Lally

Blair for the costumes. She's a stickler for authenticity, so, Romy, no cutting off your hair until she's seen you! I'm starting to audition for the rest of the cast next week, so I'll be busy until we meet again on the fourth of next month at nine-thirty sharp!'

'Make it ten, Paul!' Simon complained, 'I can't possibly make Brixton at that time through the rush hour!'

Everyone laughed, including Paul. 'That excuse won't wash! You'll be going against the traffic, but, ten it shall be if you promise to arrive on time!'

'Come and have a drink with us in the pub down the road, Romy,' Simon suggested, 'Let's get together and be cosy . . . After all we've both got to fall in love with you, and I can't do that until I know you better!'

'I can't tell you the stories going round London, dear, about how Dane and Paul found you!' Simon told her a little later at the pub, as he picked up his gin and tonic to toast her. 'We're both dying of curiosity; we want to know how much experience you've had at treading the boards!'

'They found me singing in a night club with four other girls!' she answered demurely.

'How too appropiate, darling! But have you done any stage work at all?'

'No!' She decided to share her secret fears with them. 'To be honest, when I heard about both of you I was terrified. I've been going to acting classes, but I'm afraid I might let you down!'

Mark patted her gently on the arm and comforted her. 'My dear girl! Don't start selling yourself short. Dane and Paul wouldn't have offered you the part if they didn't think you were capable of playing it!'

'I know I have a good voice,' Romy told them, still troubled, 'but I don't know if I can act.'

'All you've got to do is to believe in

Giselle, then you'll find it a breeze!' Mark told her.

'I hope you're right!' she answered, with feeling.

'He is!' Simon answered for him, 'and anyway, if you have problems you know where to come for help, now!'

Both men raised their glasses to her, and Romy flushed with pleasure. 'You're both very kind! Thanks!' She felt suddenly warm and comforted. They were being so nice to her, it helped to make up for the horrid feeling of emptiness that swept over her whenever she heard Dane's name mentioned.

'Where do you live?' Romy asked Mark shyly.

Simon interrupted. 'In a bloody great mansion in Chiswick! The fruits of success are sweet, aren't they, Mark?'

'I've worked hard enough for them!' Mark said, tranquilly, 'Your turn will come dear boy! Anyway, what's wrong with that flat of yours? It looked pretty good to me last time I was there!'

Simon grinned at him. 'I'm not complaining!'

'I should think not indeed! How's the delectable Penny?'

'Still delectable!' Simon turned to Romy, 'which reminds me! We are having a party this Saturday, so why don't you come? It will give you a chance to meet lots of people in the business. Penny's a dancer and is used to our crazy life, and I think you two would get on . . . ' He took out a card and scribbled his name and address on it. 'Don't lose it! We're ex-directory . . . ' He gave her another blinding smile. 'Everyone's dying to meet you, so you should have a good time.'

Romy stood up. 'I've got to go; Alistair is expecting me.'

Simon gave her a grin. 'I'll see you to the studio, darling! He wants me as well later this afternoon, and I'll enjoy hearing you sing again.'

★ ★ ★

Tara had left the mews house clean and tidy, so Romy had little to do except unpack her clothes and put them away. Even the large double bed had been made up with clean linen. Romy sat on the soft duvet, her hand gently stroking the cover, a smile curving the corners of her mouth. She'd never owned a double bed in her life.

That immediately conjured up the thought of Dane and what heaven it would be to wake up next to him, his dark head on the pillow, his smooth brown body next to hers . . . Furious with herself, she wrenched her thoughts away, determinedly opening cupboards and thoroughly exploring her new home before settling down to make a list of all the things she would need.

She was sitting at the round table, which, with a couple of chairs, fitted into the bow window of the sitting-room when she was disturbed by the door-bell.

'Miss Brooke?' queried a delivery man. He was carrying an enormous bowl of beautifully arranged summer flowers.

'Oh, how lovely!' she exclaimed, as he handed it to her.

'There's more to come, Miss!' he warned, as she turned to place them on the table behind her. Three times he returned, and she began to feel slightly bewildered at the selection of flowers and plants. A miniature rose bush, covered with pale pink flowers, in a matching ceramic pot was from Mary and Mark Haslam, welcoming her to her new home. 'Oh, how kind!' she spoke out loud, touched almost to tears as she went on reading. The bowl of African violets was from Scotty, and the big bouquet of cut flowers from Simon and Penny, but the huge bowl of flowers was from Dane.

She pulled out the envelope and the wire to which it was attached. Somehow she knew that large, bold writing of her name was in his hand. Inside were two carefully folded pieces of paper; she opened them and read first: 'Welcome to your new home, I hope this will remind you of your time at Grâcedieu. The nightingales sing alone now . . . '

Her eyes misted with tears as she looked at the thin, manuscript paper, covered with Dane's writing and the notes of a song. Intrigued, she read the words. He had put her song with the nightingale to music, written it just for her, with her name across the top of the paper. Her heart began to swell with happiness. He must have forgiven her, and be fond of her, to have given her this. She longed to try and play the notes; if she hurried and left now, she would be able to get to the studios where she worked with Alistair Gethin. There was a small practice room which she could use. It suddenly became important to waste no more time, so grabbing her coat and bag, she left the house. The next time she met Dane she intended to sing it to him, and as he was now back in London she had to hurry.

She woke up slightly disappointed the next morning; there had been no call from Dane or anyone else. It was Simon's party that evening, and she would have to buy a new dress. It was important that she looked her best tonight, both for her sake and Dane's.

Much later she returned to the house, carefully carrying a large bag. When she was ready she twirled slowly in front of the full-length mirror in her room, pleased with the result. Strapless white silk, swathed, the dress clung to her like a second skin until just below the hips where it flared out, the short skirt covered in spangled circles of vivid colours. Violet, red, electric blue, the shimmering effect was eye-catching. A matching silk shawl, she wore loosely tied around her shoulders. Her skin still glowed smoothly warm from her holiday in France, and her stockings, cobwebby and fine, had been chosen to enhance her tan. Her sandals were designed to match the dress.

It was not a dress for the faint-hearted, it fairly shrieked for attention, and her make-up was considerably more dramatic than normal, her large expressive eyes dominating her face. 'Three short months ago I wouldn't have dared walk into a room dressed like this!' she thought with amusement, 'but I suppose that's what this party is really all about. I'm going there tonight to see and be seen; Dane Goodman's latest star-to-be!'

She timed her arrival to be late, so her entrance would have the fullest impact on Simon's guests, and she wasn't disappointed in their reaction. In fact she decided that this was the best party she had ever been to. Eye-catching she might be in her dress, but it didn't take her long to see that it certainly wasn't outrageous compared to what some of the other girls were wearing! Soon she was the gratifying centre of a group of professionals. Chips Grant soon attached himself firmly to her side pointing people out to her, introducing her to well-known faces in the business.

Penny, who turned out to be just as nice as she had hoped from Mark's description, dragged her away to the kitchen for a chat.

'Everyone seems to want to get to know you, Romy!' she told her with mischief in her face. 'You're one of the reasons this party is being a success!'

'Have a heart!' Romy protested, 'I haven't done anything yet. I could be the greatest flop ever!'

'Oh no! Simon's pretty shrewd, you know. He's told me you've got a fantastic voice, and you obviously know how to play to a crowd! He's certain you're going to be a great star one day!'

Penny handed her a plate of quiche cut in small slices. 'Be an angel and help me pass those round, will you? You've been monopolised long enough by Chips; it's about time you had a change of scene! Dane's arrived at long last as well as Hugh Beamish and Stevie Acton. Hugh wants to hear you sing. Will you mind giving an impromptu concert?'

Romy nearly dropped the plate. 'Dane? Is he here?'

'Yes, he arrived some time ago. You will sing for us, won't you?'

This was what it was all about. If she sang Dane's solo for Giselle then the buzz was sure to go out that Dane had another hit on his hands. She was aware that the people she had met this evening were intensely curious to know what 'Queen' was all about. She followed Penny back into the big room, smiling at vaguely familiar faces, until she found herself next to Dane.

He was standing with his back towards her, one arm around a tall blonde girl. The black dress she was wearing appeared to have no back at all; her skin looked smooth and honey-gold.

'Dane!' Penny attracted his attention. 'I've managed to get Romy away from her crowd of admirers, and she says she'll sing for us!' His arm dropped quickly away from the blonde's back as he turned quickly to face her.

'Hi!' He leaned forward to give her a conventional kiss on the cheek, 'Had a good holiday?'

Romy pulled herself together. 'Great, thank you, Dane.'

She was rather pleased to notice that the blonde's face wasn't up to her figure. Rather protuberant round blue eyes, heavily made-up, and a full, sulky mouth which hid enormous teeth looked slightly incongruous in her large, rather bony face.

'Have you met Bella?' Dane enquired, idly, 'She's playing the lead in the latest Ayckbourne play.'

'No . . . ' she held out her hand, 'hello!'

Bella took it, 'Hi! I gather you're going to take this gorgeous man away from me and sing to us all?'

'That seems to be the idea . . . ' Her eyes sought his for confirmation, but he wasn't looking at her.

'It won't take long, darling . . . ' He gave Bella a warm smile, 'so don't run away just yet, will you?'

Romy felt as if she had been slapped in the face, and turned away rather blindly. She must have been mad to think that after they parted that last time that anything had changed between them. Why he should have bothered to write a song for her was a puzzle she would do well to forget. It was a brittle smile she turned towards him as he took her arm and led her to the piano.

'Thank you for the flowers, Dane . . . and for the song.'

He turned to study her face intently. 'Did you like it?'

'I shall have to wait until I can find a piano.'

'Don't give me that! You can read music perfectly well.'

'I'll look at it properly tomorrow, then,' she answered lightly, 'I've been rather busy the last two days, as you can imagine. I'm sorry if I've offended you by not studying it carefully before this.'

'I don't think you're the slightest bit sorry!' he snapped, 'so why pretend? You are behaving exactly like a spoilt child again . . .'

'Just what do you mean?' she hissed under her breath.

He smiled at her. 'You know perfectly well what I mean! You don't like me paying attention to anyone else when you're around, do you?' He saw the flash of temper in her eyes, and his smile was mocking as he continued quietly: 'Don't forget you are as good as on a stage here tonight!'

His words pulled her up sharply, and as he sat down at the piano, she gave a brilliant smile to everyone standing around, much quieter now.

So she sang, and she put her heart into every word as she told of the agonising pain love can sometimes bring, her own troubled feelings adding extra pathos to the words and music; and at the end of it, she was rewarded by a stunned silence for a few seconds.

The roar of appreciation seemed even louder to her after the earlier silence; her eyes were glistening with unshed tears.

'My God! If she can do that on the stage every night . . . ' She heard Stevie Acton's words to Hugh Beamish, and her heart filled with gratitude. Those two were the best-known theatrical impresarios in London and if they thought she was great, then she had nothing more to fear. Dane was watching her, an arrested expression in his eyes, as if she had somehow surprised him. He read the question in hers, and said quietly, 'Thank you.'

Singing had made her forget what had happened before, and obviously he felt the same way. They were being besieged to perform something else, but Dane stood up and firmly shut the piano, a good-humoured grin on his face. 'No, no more! You'll have to wait until opening night to hear the rest!'

He went to get a drink for Romy. She could have gone on singing all night, but Chips brought her back to earth. 'He's a clever bastard, isn't he? Some of the most influential people in show business are here tonight, and he's made sure he's got them all eating out of his hand; and set your feet firmly on the first rung of the ladder to success at the same time!'

# 6

The party at Simon's flat seemed to spell out the parameters of Romy's relationship with Dane. Professionally they worked very well together, but in private they seemed destined to remain at odds.

She wrote a shy little note to him apologising for her behaviour at the party and thanking him for the flowers and the nightingale's song, but he ignored her friendly overture. She kept the manuscript with her other meagre treasures in an old-fashioned tin box that had belonged to her father, and as she locked it away, it seemed to her that she was also symbolically locking away her own hopes and dreams.

As far as her work was concerned, she grew more and more confident. Both Alistair and Dane worked with her on the score until she became totally

117

familiar with it. Her voice stretched and deepened, surprising her by its richness and strength. She said as much to Dane one day.

'It doesn't surprise me at all!' he had answered, smiling at her. 'I always knew this would happen. The only thing that does surprise me is that you didn't choose to go for a career in opera. Your mother must have been a remarkable woman — I would have liked to have met her, because it's obvious she knew very well what you were capable of. Was she really just a gifted amateur, Romy?'

She couldn't stop the burning sweep of colour over her face. 'No, I promise you my mother never sang professionally, but she did train as a singer . . . That's why she knew how to t-teach me!' she stuttered.

'I get the distinct impression that you are hiding something from me!' he answered grimly.

'No! Both my parents were teachers . . . There isn't anything else to tell!'

He stared down into her frantically pleading eyes, his own hard, the brows slightly frowning. 'I wish I could believe you . . . I know very little about you, Romy! You are extraordinarily intriguing, you know . . . You never talk much about your past life; if you weren't so young I'd almost believe you are hiding some guilty secret!'

Her voice was dull, almost lifeless as she answered. 'My life has been very ordinary, Dane, boring really . . . You wouldn't be interested in hearing about it.'

'Why so sure, little one?' He picked up one of her hands, holding it gently. 'Both Paul and I would always be interested to hear more about our future star!'

Tears were prickling uncomfortably behind her eyes. It would be so easy to fall for the warmth and lazy charm in his voice. He just wanted to find out more about her in case there was something in her past that could damage the show. She pulled her hand out of his, 'You've nothing to worry about! I've done nothing in my life that I need be ashamed of!'

'That wasn't what I meant!' He, too, was now angry. 'Why can't you stop behaving like a hedgehog whenever I ask you anything? I appreciate your wish to keep your private life private, but surely even you can't be naïve enough to think that the press won't dig deep into your past life once you're a star?'

'No, I'm not that naïve!' she shouted, 'but just because I've accepted the part of Giselle, that does not give you the right to dig into my private life! Stop leaning on me, Dane! I don't need your interest in anything except my professional life!'

'If that's the way you want it, then that's all you're going to get!' he shouted back at her, before leaving the room, slamming the door behind him.

Alone, she collapsed onto the floor, wondering what demon had possessed her to repel his kindness, because this time she was sure he'd really got the message.

After that, he left her more in Alistair Gethin's hands, almost as if he could no longer be bothered with her. He wasn't even there when she went to the recording studio to cut her first disc. That was the first time she had sung with a full orchestra, and she found it impossible to control her elation as she allowed her voice to soar higher and higher as she lost herself in the beautiful music Dane had written.

Alistair laughed at her when she tried to apologise to him afterwards.

'Don't worry! I thought that might happen . . . We didn't have any problem keeping up with you, did we?'

She grinned. 'No, none at all . . . '

'You've just collected a few more fans. Look at them!' She saw the orchestra had stood up and were gently applauding her. 'They don't often accord that privilege to the people they accompany,' he grinned,

'I can see they hope we're going to make the number one spot!'

It was a strange experience to hear herself on the master tape at the recording studio, but by the end of a hard day's work she had to admit that her voice sounded good. None of them seemed in any doubt that her first release would climb the charts quickly, and her career would soon have a new dimension. More and more she realised how much she owed Dane for giving her those extra months to work up to what seemed like certain success.

Paul Saint's likable young assistant Chips Grant had become perhaps her closest companion. He turned out to be a tower of strength, always ready to help her. She learnt more about the world of theatre from him than any class could have taught her. He was amusing, understanding, yet also undemanding, and she knew his great ambition was to direct a production like 'Queen' himself.

'Maybe I'll direct you one day,

who knows?' he told her happily as they walked one Sunday morning in St. James's Park with a bag of bread to feed the ducks. This had become almost a ritual with them both now, the Sunday morning walk, then returning to Romy's house where she cooked them both lunch.

'I hope so, why not?' she agreed happily, 'You know me so well now that you probably know what I'm capable of more than myself!'

He gave her a sudden curious look. 'Do you think so? I don't! You're a funny girl in some ways; easy on the surface to know and like, but underneath there's another person, and that's why you fascinate me so much.'

Without thinking, Romy answered, 'Dane said that to me as well . . . '

'Dane! Well, I'm not surprised, I've always thought him a very clever man . . . ' He gave her a quick, sideways glance. 'You two have got something going together, haven't you?'

'No, we have not! Honestly; Chips,

123

how can you suggest such a thing?'

'Easily!' came the quick response, 'It's the way you two watch each other, particularly when you both think you aren't being observed!'

Surprised, she looked at him. 'Dane watches me?'

'Yup! And he's been giving me some pretty funny looks just lately.'

'There really isn't anything going on between us, I promise you, Chips!'

'All right, all right! I can see I've put my foot in it! But I'm not really surprised, because you are a very fascinating lady!'

She answered stiffly. 'Don't exaggerate! There's not much to know about me . . . My past really rather uninteresting. Anyway, does anyone ever appear totally open, like the pages in a book? For instance, there's masses of things I don't know about you!'

'I think you're going to be a great star one day, and nobody gets to that position by being just a sweet, nice, little girl! There has to be a great deal more to you than a lot of ambition!'

'Thanks for the vote of confidence, I hope you're right. I don't see myself yet as at all special, I promise you . . . '

'No, you wouldn't! But then that's one of your charms, isn't it?'

She stopped by the side of the lake and threw some of the stale bread to the greedy ducks. 'By the way, have they found an understudy for me yet?'

'I think it's down to a choice between two . . . One of them is the Swedish girl from that German pop group that made the charts last month 'Reflections'.'

'I remember,' she sounded relieved, 'she's a very good singer. I think . . . '

'Yes, she is, but she's not such a good actress unfortunately.'

'And the other?' she enquired idly.

'I don't know much about her, except that she's English, and belongs to some minor operatic company. They are going to choose tomorrow.'

'Which one does Dane want?'

'I honestly don't know, Romy! It's

been almost as hard to find an understudy as it was to find you!'

'Well, whoever they choose, I don't intend to let them take over my role! So, if they've got any ideas about instant stardom standing in for me, they can forget it!'

Chips looked at her with astonishment. 'Hey! That doesn't sound like you at all. You've got nothing to worry about, whoever they find won't be as good as you!'

She was suddenly a bit ashamed of her outburst. 'I'm sorry, blame it on my insecurity . . . '

'Insecurity? Whatever for? You've done brilliantly so far. Paul's terribly pleased with you and you know perfectly well you've got both Mark and Simon eating out of your hand!'

She could see she had again aroused his curiosity, so gave him a big smile, and until he left after lunch she made strenuous efforts to divert his attention away from her. She was free to follow her own track.

She guessed it was because the young assistant was more than a bit fond of her that he had the perception to see what she hoped no-one else had begun to suspect. She would have to be much more careful in the future. She belatedly realised she had been using him without the slightest thought for his feelings. He wasn't in love with her yet, but soon could be if she continued to see him as much as she had done.

She went to the theatre the next morning, full of a dull foreboding, and found it hard to concentrate on one of the dance routines. Mags Bond, the girl in charge of all the choreography, nearly lost her temper with her, when for the fifth time in succession she missed her chalked place on the stage.

'For God's sake, Romy! It's three steps between each turn, not four, you idiot! You've got to end up by the third table on the right, where Simon will be sitting. Then you sing to him for the first time, get it?'

'I'm sorry, Mags, I just can't seem

to concentrate this morning!'

'You're telling me! Look, take a break for ten minutes. I'll work the girls alone till you're ready to try it again.'

Moodily, Romy stepped into her track suit, careful not to allow herself to get chilled. She was wearing no make-up, and her hair was drawn back from her face in a simple ponytail. All in all it could hardly have been a worse moment to be summoned to Dane's office by Paul Saint.

'Great, you're free then! Dane wants you to come and meet someone who could be your understudy.'

Apprehensively, she followed him to Dane's office. Paul opened the door, motioning her to precede him into the room. Her eyes fastened quickly onto Dane before turning reluctantly to meet the cat-like smile of her cousin Elizabeth. Dane's watchful eyes turned wary as they took in the expression of shock on Romy's face as she looked at the other girl.

'Hello, Romy! Dad and I were delighted when we heard you'd managed to land on your feet. We'd been wondering what had happened to you this last eighteen months.'

Romy's face shuttered at these words, and she turned on her heel and left the room, ignoring the shock on Paul's face and Dane's furious shout. She broke into a run, desperate to get away, nearly knocking Chips flat in her mad dash for her dressing-room. Once there, she bolted the door, then collapsed in a heap on the stool in front of the big mirror.

'Romy! Let me in this minute . . . ' She recognised the voice as Dane's. For a moment she ignored him, but the assault on the door could not be ignored. With a face of stone she got up and unlocked it, standing aside, as the angry man erupted into her room.

'Just what the hell was that all about?' he snarled at her.

'I don't like your choice of under-study,' she answered, her voice cold.

'Bloody hell! I went to immense trouble to get her here this morning just because she was your cousin!'

'You should have listened to me when I told you I had no family!' she snapped.

'Why, Romy? Why?'

'Why?' She heavily and sarcastically underlined the word, 'Why should I tell you? My private life is private, and I intend to see that it stays that way!'

'It's a bit late for that line, my dear! Your cousin has already favoured me with her version of why you ran away!'

'Then you don't need to know any more from me, do you?'

He banged his hand down hard on the dressing-table so that everything on it jumped. 'Stop playing games! I don't want to be used as a pawn in your family feud! I think you owe me an explanation?'

'I don't want to discuss it. I have never wanted anyone poking around in my family affairs!'

He lifted a weary hand to his face. 'Don't you understand the first thing about this game? When you become a star, then everything that the press can dig up about you, your family, anything! will become news. This . . . disagreement with your family will be blazoned all over the gutter press!'

'Let it!' she retorted scornfully.

'You can't mean that! You have no idea, no conception of the power of the press these days! For God's sake let's try to sort this thing out now, Romy, otherwise you'll get horribly hurt!'

'I don't think it will be me who is hurt!'

'You obstinate fool! Why won't you listen?'

'Why did you listen to her?' she demanded fiercely. 'Why did you have to pick on her? Was it to spite me?'

'For heaven's sake! Nobody could have been more surprised than me when I heard she was your cousin! You told me, if you remember, that you

131

had no family. What did you expect me to do when she came out with this information? Use your head! Her voice has the same quality as yours, she can act . . . '

'She's had plenty of practice!' she interjected bitterly.

Dane looked at her in a considering way. 'I think you are being a bit silly about all of this you know . . . There is no question of her taking your place. Elizabeth has said nothing to us about any family row, just that her father was upset when you left their home . . . They've apparently been looking for you for some time . . . '

'Like hell they were! If they'd looked they'd have found me soon enough, you can be sure of that! They must have had a nasty shock when they found out I had the lead in your latest musical!'

Dane took her hands, holding them in a strong clasp. 'Tell me! Tell me what's behind all this!'

She shut her eyes in a kind of

agony. He was so hard to resist when he looked at her like that. 'I can't, Dane . . . '

He gave an impatient sigh, dropping her hands, and his voice was hard as he said: 'I'm not going to stop considering her for the part you know. You've given me no good reason for doing so . . . ' Her eyes lifted and held his dark ones. He swore loudly. 'Don't think you can intimidate me! I mean what I say. If you won't give me one good reason for your dislike, then she stays! Do you understand?'

'Yes, I understand. You want Elizabeth to be my understudy, don't you? You've wanted it all along, and even if I had given you good reasons for not having her you wouldn't have considered them good enough, would you?'

She could see the swift tide of anger that swept over him, tinging his cheeks with red. 'At least I could see she was an adult, which is more than can be said for you!'

'You wouldn't have given me the lead as Giselle if you really thought of me as a child!' she taunted.

'Wouldn't I? But I hope you've noticed that I've taken good care to cut you out of my private life, because I'm not interested in playing with children!' There was a cruel smile on his face as he watched the play of emotions on hers. 'I think I shall enjoy getting to know Elizabeth. Somehow I don't think she'll tell me as many lies as you have! I've already found out that you are Dame Alicia Hepburn's granddaughter, which explains your voice and your undoubted theatrical talent!'

'Then why don't you offer her the part of Giselle? She'd jump at the chance of playing her!'

'Now you're being childish again! As childish as you were when you denied to me that you had any theatrical talent in your family, apart from yourself! You realise that all of this would have come out in the press don't you? Paul and I would have looked

134

like fools when the story broke, which it inevitably would! I suggest that if you have any more dark secrets which you aren't willing to confide in me, then you tell Paul. There's too much riding on this show for the threat of bad publicity about the leading lady to upset the backers!'

'There's isn't anything else to know!' she protested, 'and anyway I can't see many of your public knowing anything about my grandmother!'

'You really enjoy hitting below the belt don't you?' he hissed back at her. 'So! Now we know what you really think about my music. That it's beneath the attention of any really serious musician!'

'I didn't say that!'

'You didn't have to, did you?'

'I didn't mean it either! You've just jumped to another wrong conclusion!' she snapped back.

He shrugged his shoulders and moved towards the door. 'By the way I suppose it is hopeless to suggest to you that you offer your cousin the spare room in your house?'

'Absolutely hopeless!' she agreed through gritted teeth. 'Anyway how do you know there is a spare bedroom?'

'I happen to own the freehold!' He gave her a last malicious smile before leaving her at last.

She sank down onto the stool while her thoughts raced around inside her head.

She'd always accepted that Uncle Max would find her, but she'd hoped it would be after her success, not like this. Her uncle and his daughter Elizabeth had gone out of their way to try and ensure that any singing success should never be hers. A strange, jealous obsession that had started almost as soon as she had been born, just two years after Elizabeth, and balancing it, her mother's almost equal obsession that she should succeed and triumph over her cousin.

The root of the trouble had been her maternal grandmother. Dame Alicia

Hepburn had been a formidable prima donna with an uncertain temperament which had occasionally made her as much hated in the musical world as her public had loved her. She had never forgiven Romy's mother for two reasons. First her voice had not been quite good enough for a career, and secondly she had married a simple schoolmaster.

Her son had been clever enough to marry a young singer of whom his mother approved. It was said Dame Alicia intended to train her to take her place on the world stage, but the young girl had died of some obscure complication only two months after her daughter's birth.

Gossip had it that she had died of exhaustion, as her mother-in-law had not allowed her to rest properly after the birth of her child. On her death, Dame Alicia had concentrated all her attention on her first granddaughter.

Quite a long time went by before she acknowledged that she had another granddaughter who could also sing, possibly rather better than Elizabeth. Romy had refused to change her name to Hepburn, also to allow her grandmother to train her voice.

Contrary to all expectations her behaviour rather amused the old lady. She paid for Elizabeth to go to the Royal College of Music, and had intended to do the same for Romy. Unfortunately Dame Alicia died the summer before Romy was due to leave school. She left no provision for Romy's training.

What she did set out in her will was a nasty shock for Elizabeth and her father. Whichever of the two girls first played a leading role in the professional theatre would inherit the bulk of her estate, and her collection of musical memorabilia. Her house, and a small annuity were all she left her son. Her daughter, Romy's mother, got nothing.

The unfairness had made Romy's mother all the more determined that it should be her daughter who benefited.

The death of her parents changed that. She discovered her home had been only rented, and she would be lucky to be left with a couple of thousand pounds. She would be unable to train as a singer unless her uncle could help her.

It didn't take long for her to realise that they had no intention of helping her, in fact were rather pleased at the way things had turned out. They offered her a room in her grandmother's house, but she was told she would be expected to take a job to pay for her keep. Elizabeth had just been taken on by an operatic company, and her small, catlike, smile hardly left her face.

That had been the moment that Romy's determination to succeed at all costs had been born. Her grandmother's will had not specifically stated that she had to succeed in opera, so Romy had determined to succeed her way. The ill-feeling that existed between herself and her remaining family would be hard to explain to an outsider. Romy had grown up under the shadow of her mother's bitterness. Part of her was easy and uncomplicated like her father, but the other part, the hidden self that she tried to suppress, was ruthless and tough like her grandmother.

What lengths would her uncle and cousin go to to stop her inheriting? They must have had a bad shock when they found out what she had been doing.

# 7

Romy found Paul Saint waiting for her when she had finished her routines with the other dancers. Matters could not be left as they were, but what was she to tell him? He wouldn't believe her if she hinted that she was afraid of what might happen to her. There was so much money at stake from her grandmother's will that there was every chance that her family might not be able to resist the temptation to even up the odds a little in their favour.

Dane had hurt her so badly by his championing of Elizabeth that she was determined for the moment to tell him nothing. Since that moment alone together in France she found herself on the defensive with him.

Uncle Max and Elizabeth had tried to make her into a modern Cinderella, but she didn't have the right sort of temperament to accept her fate meekly, so she had left to make her own way. She felt proud that she was so near to success. She felt even more proud that it had been achieved without the use of the name 'Hepburn'. Dame Alicia had been a wicked, unforgiving old woman, and Romy guessed that she had enjoyed putting her family at logger-heads with each other.

She followed Paul silently towards his office. He shut the door firmly, and Romy was far too engrossed with her own thoughts to notice the attention they were both getting from the girls working there.

'Well, Romy? Are you going to tell me what all this fuss has been about?'

She gave him a tired smile. 'I wish I could, Paul, but it's such a long complicated story, that even if I told you, I don't think you'd believe me at the end.' Nervously she rubbed her hands against her arms, as if trying to comfort herself. 'Couldn't you please accept that it would be a disaster for me, and my cousin Elizabeth, if she became my understudy?'

'Why make my life more difficult than it is, Romy? Dane wants a reason from you, you know that.'

She wriggled uncomfortably under his hard stare.

'Would you accept that there are very real family reasons why it would be a disaster?' she pleaded.

'I would, Romy, but it isn't just me, is it? There are the backers, as well as Dane . . . '

She gave a sigh. 'All right! Tell Dane I'll try to give him my reasons . . . '

'Promise?' he said, sharply.

'Yes, I promise,' she agreed, tiredly. She owed it to them to tell the truth.

He gave her a smile. 'It's a good thing that Dane and I agreed that it would be better not to have Elizabeth as your understudy!'

Shock made her eyes appear enormous.

'Dane and you . . . You've both d-decided . . . ' she stammered, unable to get the words out. He gave her a surprisingly kind smile.

'It isn't a very good idea to upset one's leading lady.'

'But, Dane! He said he had absolutely decided on Elizabeth!'

'You made him lose his temper!'

'What about Elizabeth? I mean, didn't she mind?'

'She didn't appear to! Anyway Dane has taken her out to lunch. She hasn't been asked to sign a contract.'

'I don't understand! If she didn't want the part, then why was she here this morning?'

'Oh, Dane heard her sing at some private party. He was struck by a similarity between your voices, and told her about his problems in finding an understudy for you. I think he had quite a job persuading her to come here. I gather she thinks of herself as a serious, operatic singer, and that all this,' he waved an expansive hand, 'is rather beneath her.'

'She would!' Romy interjected bitterly.

'From what I overhead this morning

I gather she may have the chance of Desdemona in 'Otello' in Munich next year!'

Romy's hands twisted anxiously in her lap. 'Do you know when?'

'No, my dear, I don't.' He looked at her with undisguised surprise. She was concentrating hard; her brow furrowed with tiny lines. 'But if that's the case,' she suddenly burst out, 'then there could never be any question of Elizabeth taking the part of my understudy! She would never have agreed to that if there was a chance of her singing Desdemona!'

'As to that, I wouldn't know. I thought we had both agreed on Sonja Birgl. She's not a good actress but she sings and dances well, and is the front singer for the pop group 'Reflections'. She doesn't like the touring.'

'Are you sure there's no question of my cousin as understudy?' she queried, still not quite believing what Paul had told her.

'Absolutely sure! Dane doesn't want

you to be upset. My guess is that he only tried to persuade her just because she *was* your cousin. I hope you're feeling happier now that everything has been sorted out?' She gave a strangely negative gesture with one hand.

'Of course, Paul! You've been very kind. I'm sorry I made such a scene this morning, but, well, the circumstances were awkward to say the least!'

'Listen, Romy! I don't know what's gone wrong between you and Dane, but you should trust him! I know he has your best interests at heart . . . He really twisted Tara's arm to let you take the rest of the lease on the mews, and he's not likely to serve you a back-handed turn. He's gone to tremendous lengths to make sure you are a success in this production, in fact we've all taken a big gamble on it. So don't fight him too hard at the moment, he's got enough problems of his own.'

She was very late leaving the theatre that evening. To add to her miseries,

146

it had started to rain so she was forced to catch the tube because there were no taxis. It was nearly dark by the time she turned into the mews, and her jeans and trainers were wet and uncomfortable. The cobbles felt slippery under her feet as she walked.

She heard a car start up at the far end of the mews, the engine revving up into a snarl. Startled, she was dazzled as the headlights were switched full on. She threw up a hand to protect her eyes from the glare, and heard Dane's voice calling her name, on a note of desperation.

'Jump, Romy! For God's sake, jump!'

The car was almost on her. She threw herself sideways, her ribs connecting painfully with a large wooden tub full of flowers. She rolled over and over, curling her body into a ball. Her head was full of noise, and it hurt her to breathe. Terror held her in the position, as she waited to feel her body crushed under the wheels.

She felt herself picked up by two strong arms; there was the sound of concerned voices, a bright light shone in her eyes, and she was being carried by someone away from the horror of the last few moments. Thankful, she turned her face into a warm chest and allowed the spinning sensation in her head to float her away into nothingness.

She woke up slowly, in her own bed, but with a strange face bending over her.

'Miss Brooke?'

A spasm of pain had her catching her breath. A hand lightly held her wrist. 'What's happened?' she gasped.

'Don't try and talk now . . . ' the voice was kind and reassuring, 'There's nothing to worry about . . . '

Romy's head felt full of cotton wool, 'Dane . . . ' she muttered.

'Don't worry, Mr Goodman's here . . . Now I'm going to give you an injection to make you sleep — you'll feel more like yourself in the morning.'

Dane was here, that was all right then. Her lids felt far too heavy to stay open. She gave herself up to the blessed relief of sleep.

Romy woke up early the next morning, feeling sore and uncomfortable. It hurt her to breathe, and she guessed she must have severely bruised herself against the tub of flowers. On turning her head, she saw Dane lying back in a chair next to her.

He was deeply asleep, his head turned slightly towards hers, his thick dark lashes lying in a heavy curve on his cheeks. He looked frightfully uncomfortable and very tired. He must have stayed with her all night. Of course! She remembered now, it had been he who had called on her to jump. That car . . . Had it really been trying to knock her down? She remembered the petrified fear that had kept her standing there until she had responded to Dane's voice. She tried to move her bruised body out of the bed and into the bathroom. Who had undressed her last night, Dane or the doctor?

Alone in the bathroom, still not able to stand up straight, she peered into the mirror. She looked awful. There was a large purple bruise on one side of her forehead and her skin looked pasty-white. Her eyes seemed to have sunk into her head. Her body ached too much for her to feel up to doing anything about it. She cleaned her teeth, with slightly trembling hands. Wincing, she managed to pull up her nightdress to see one side of her ribs covered with ugly bruising. Shocked, she let the nightie fall again. God! It wasn't surprising she felt as if she could hardly move.

Her bed had never seemed more attractive; she felt like an old, arthritic woman as she tried to avoid Dane's chair.

'Romy!' He was awake in an instant. 'What are you doing out of bed? Why didn't you wake me?' He stood up rather stiffly. 'You are an idiot! Doctor

Craig didn't want you to move until he had been into see you . . . ' He helped her into the bed. 'You poor child!' he said softly, as she winced, 'that was a hell of a thing to happen!'

He helped to put several pillows behind her back. 'Doctor Craig told me you would feel better if you tried to rest, sitting up,' he explained, 'He'll be back here soon. I'm afraid you've got to go to hospital to have those ribs X-rayed.'

By taking shallow little breaths Romy was able to move and talk without too much pain. 'It doesn't look as if you've had an exactly comfortable night either!' she managed.

'I couldn't leave you alone, could I?'

'It's very kind of you,' she agreed, 'You should have made up the bed in the spare room!'

'I wanted to be on hand in case you needed me . . . ' He rubbed a hand over his rough face, then grinned. 'I hope you've got some of those disposable razors in the bathroom.'

'You're in luck!' she answered quietly, trying not to let her emotions show too clearly on her face. She was so grateful to him for staying with her, that her eyes blurred a little with unshed tears.

'Hey! You look as if you could do with a cup of tea and something to eat!'

'Wouldn't you rather have a bath first?'

She couldn't mistake the tenderness on his face as he looked down at her. 'No way! Breakfast first for you, then my bath!'

By the time Doctor Craig returned she was feeling a little less weak and dizzy. The hot tea having revived her more than anything else.

The doctor gave her a thorough examination before saying, 'Well, I think you've been lucky, Miss Brooke. Your ribs are severely bruised, but I don't think you have broken any of them. All the same, you must have an X-ray to make sure . . . There's no question of you going back to rehearsal for some time yet!'

'But, Doctor, I must!' she protested, 'I can't hold up the whole cast of 'Queen' just for a few bruised ribs!'

He gave her a quizzical look over the half-moon glasses he wore. 'When were you thinking of returning? This afternoon?'

'No . . . I don't think I'd be much use this afternoon, but surely in a couple of days?'

'It'll be more like a couple of weeks before you'll get your body moving comfortably again!' he answered sharply. 'You'll be of no use in the theatre until you've recovered.'

Miserably she subsided, making no more protests. 'Mr Goodman is going to drive you over to the hospital later this morning, and I've already written out a prescription for some painkillers . . . ' He gave her detailed instructions as to what she was, and more importantly what she was not to do for the next few days.

He left her then, and wondered if Dane was going to be furious with her for holding up the rehearsals. It was some time before he reappeared, and she heard him on the telephone, making several calls by the sound of it.

She started another train of thought. How could the car driver not have seen her in his headlights? He had made no move to brake, or avoid her . . . The image of her grandmother came into her mind, old and imperious. Surely this had nothing to with her will?

She heard Dane's feet on the stairs; then he knocked, and entered her room. 'Right! Scotty's coming to take care of you until we can find someone suitable from the agency . . . Hey! what's the matter, Romy?' His eyes, took in the tear stains on her cheeks. 'Tears? Now what have you got to cry about?'

She shut her eyes to stop the treacherous flow. 'I'm so sorry, Dane . . . Will it really be all right? The show, I mean?'

'Of course it will, you idiot! It'll give Sonja Birgl a chance to find her feet . . . Anyway, what's two weeks? Thanks to you, we're considerably more advanced than either Paul or I hoped to be at this stage.'

She smiled faintly at his words. 'If I'd been a bit quicker on my feet last night, then you wouldn't be put to so much trouble now!'

His eyes darkened at the mention of last night. 'Forget it, Romy! It was a nasty experience, but we'll probably never know the true reason behind that idiot's behaviour — he was probably high on drugs or something . . . '

'He? Did you see it was a man?'

'Yes, I saw . . . But I was in too much of a funk about you to have taken numbers or anything practical like that!'

She heard the self-disgust in his voice. 'If it wasn't for your voice yelling at me to jump, I'd probably have been hit!'

He shrugged his shoulders. 'Maybe . . . '

The injection the doctor had given her was making her feel better. 'About yesterday,' she started, then seeing his frown said, 'No! not that, earlier . . . I owe you an apology . . . ' The sound of the doorbell interrupted her.

'Good! That'll be Scotty.' He bounded down the stairs to let in his secretary.

Dane drove Romy to the hospital. Doctor Craig was right, there were no cracked ribs, just bruising, but she was given no chance of telling Dane about her family. He seemed determined to stop her telling him anything but the merest commonplace, and she was too unsure of herself to persist.

Scotty, of course, was her usual efficient self, but she was genuinely horrified when she saw the extent of Romy's bruising. 'Heavens! That must hurt . . . No wonder the boss was in such a state! He was in such a flap last night. I've never known him like that before!'

'Police?' Romy's voice was suddenly sharp.

'Yes! One of your neighbours saw what happened, and called them, but of course no-one got the number of the car, so there was very little they could do. I believe someone's coming round to see you later today . . . '

'I see . . . ' Romy was thoughtful. Dane had left to go to the theatre, assuring both of them he would be back before too long. Scotty soon left her alone to rest.

The police! What if they asked her if she knew of anyone who was likely to do her harm? If only Dane had allowed her to speak to him seriously this morning! She desperately needed his advice, before she confided her suspicions to anyone as impersonal as the police . . . Anyway did she actually believe that Uncle Max would try to hurt her? She never once seriously considered that Elizabeth would countenance anything quite so drastic. Petty spite, yes, maybe . . . but nothing as dramatic as trying to knock her down with a car. But she was more tired than she realised, and slipped back into a light sleep.

Dane was sitting by her bed once more when she awoke. 'Hello!' he greeted her, 'feeling better?' She nodded. 'Good. We've managed to find someone to come and take care of you. Her name's Mrs Heather . . . She used to be a nurse; I think you'll like her.'

'Is it really necessary for me to have anyone here?'

'Maybe not strictly necessary, but rather nice not to be alone, I thought?'

'Is she here now?'

'No, she's coming this evening, about six o'clock I hope.'

She couldn't help saying, 'I wish you'd accept that I'm not a child, and perfectly capable of looking after myself!'

He raised his eyebrows. 'I see you're feeling better . . . ' but he allowed his face to relax in a grin.

In spite of herself, she smiled back at him, then began quickly to tell him about her family and her grandmother's will.

It was hard to read his face when she had finished, and she began nervously to pleat the duvet cover under her fingers as she waited for him to say something. She had his complete attention.

'Good God, Romy! How on earth do you think we'll keep that quiet? It's one hell of a story . . . '

'No-one will remember my name!' she protested.

He gave her a half smile. 'You'll be surprised how many people will remember you when you're famous! Also it will soon be known that you are Dame Alicia's granddaughter as well as Elizabeth . . . My God! I'm not surprised you didn't want Elizabeth as your understudy. I really put my foot in it, didn't I?'

'You weren't to know . . . '

'Are you sure about the terms of Dame Alicia's will?' he asked curiously, 'because I would have thought she would only have been interested in operatic roles, and I can't see singing the lead role in 'Queen' as exactly qualifying you to benefit.'

'I have a copy of it. It doesn't mention anything about being a specifically operatic role! Although I'm sure that's what she meant. I don't think she ever imagined either of us singing anything else!'

'So, after the opening night you are going to claim your inheritance?'

'I've thought of doing nothing else since my parents died,' she answered fiercely. 'I don't care about the money, I never did, I just don't want my greedy relations walking away with it as their right! They did their best to see that I had no chance when I was left alone. Elizabeth has had every chance. She's two years older, and her voice has been professionally trained.'

'This all explains so much about you,' he said in a relieved tone.

She turned away from him, and shut her eyes. This wasn't what she wanted to hear from him. Interested curiosity, that's all it was. 'Please, I'm still rather tired . . . '

'All right, Romy, I understand . . . But I think it would be better if you face up to the fact that the man behind the wheel of that car could have been your uncle!'

She turned a shocked face towards him. 'You're not to tell the police that!'

He folded his arms. 'Why not? It's the truth, isn't it? You were paralysed with fear when I picked you up out of the gutter last night. When I had a chance to think about it I realised your reaction had to be more than shock at narrowly escaping an accident. That's why you passed out in my arms afterwards.'

She couldn't stop the tears that began to pour down her face. 'What am I to do, Dane?' she whispered.

'Nothing! Leave it to me . . . ' His face was set in grim lines. 'I'll take care of this, and without any attendant publicity if I can help it! Is there a lot of money at stake?'

Again she nodded her head miserably. 'I think it's about three-quarters of a million . . . '

'Murder has been done for a great deal less!'

'Murder? Oh no, Dane! No, I don't think that was intended . . . Just enough of an accident to put me out of 'Queen'.'

'How important really is this money to you?'

'It isn't important at all! I never wanted the money . . . Just the chance to sing . . . '

'Do you mean that?'

She looked dazed at the fierceness of the question. 'Of course. If I had it, I would give it away! I prefer to live on what I earn. My grandmother used her wealth to cause trouble between her children! It was wicked what she did to my mother, to us all!'

'She didn't exactly have the most conciliating reputation in the musical world, did she?' Dane stood up suddenly. 'Will you trust me enough to leave this whole mess in my hands?'

She nodded her head.

'That's my girl! I'll sort this out in a civilised way, and there'll be no publicity.' The ring of the doorbell disturbed him. 'That'll probably be Mrs Heather. She did say she'd try to get here earlier if she could!' He gave her a penetrating glance. 'Don't worry any more, Romy! And try to forget what has happened.'

# 8

Romy was given plenty of time to think over the next ten days. Dane's high-handed interference in her affairs bothered her slightly although she wasn't quite sure why, because she had as good as asked for his help. He refused point-blank to tell her how he intended to resolve the problem when she tried to pin him down.

'Nature can't be hurried!' Doctor Craig told her severely one day when she begged him for an injection so that she could go back to work a bit earlier.

Mrs Heather was a tower of strength, as well as being practical and sympathetic. Romy found herself keeping open house, as most of the cast of 'Queen' managed to call round and see her. Her little house was full of flowers. Mrs Heather relished all the actors and show business people who called in to see Romy.

Her accident had been 'news'. Already her first single was climbing steadily in the charts, and the press began to take more of an interest in her. There were press releases about her future role as 'Giselle' and a number of photographs had been taken in anticipation of this moment. She photographed extremely well; she was naïvely surprised at how beautiful some of the shots made her look.

Dane always came round to the mews with other people, sometimes Paul, sometimes just Scotty, so it was impossible to ask him anything serious. Her accident with the car had been explained away as just that — there had been no hint that a darker motive could lie behind it.

The night before she was due back at the theatre, and Mrs Heather was rather sadly packing up to leave, Dane called her.

'I've ordered a car to take you

to the theatre each day, and it will collect you every evening,' he told her.

'Oh come on! That's not necessary, Dane. I can easily get taxis . . . Anyway I can't afford the luxury!'

'I thought you had agreed to let me handle things my way?' he answered, provocatively.

She thought she could detect overtones of amusement in the deep, velvety voice. 'Why should it be necessary to have a car?'

She heard the ghost of his laugh, 'Patience, Romy! These things can't always be settled as quickly as we would like.'

'I wish you would tell me what you have planned!'

'I will, when I've got everyone's agreement.'

'You seem very sure of yourself!'

'I will tell you one thing. Your cousin Elizabeth seems to be a lot more co-operative than you!'

A sudden chill ran through her. It

became of supreme importance not to let him know how his words had affected her. 'Really?'

'Yes, 'really',' he mimicked, 'now get a good night's sleep!'

Dane and Elizabeth . . . she choked back a sob; why had she never thought of that? He'd even hinted at it, when they had been having that last, ghastly row in her dressing-room.

'Hello, dear!' Mrs Heather peeped round the bedroom door, 'Sad though it is, I'm afraid I ought to be off on my travels!'

Romy turned to smile at the older woman. 'I don't know how I can thank you enough for all you've done . . . '

'You've already thanked me quite enough, and as long as you remember to send me that ticket for 'Queen of the Night' then I'm going to be the one in your debt, my dear!'

'Don't worry, Mrs Heather! You'll get two of them, I promise.'

'That'll be lovely. It's been a real pleasure looking after you. More of a holiday really for me, meeting all those lovely people!'

As Romy shut the door behind Mrs Heather, she relished the fact that she was at long last alone. Her bruises had faded, but she was now filled with another ache, an infinitely more painful experience than anything she had suffered in the last two weeks.

Back at the theatre the production was really beginning to take shape. Romy threw herself back into her work with a renewed vigour, knowing that there was time to make up.

Lally Blair had already started to make some of the wonderful figure-hugging costumes she was to wear. Her usually unmanageable hair had been expertly cut so that it hung gently onto her shoulders, just curling slightly at the ends.

Her single had now made the number one spot, and every day that went by Paul and Dane worked to weld the cast into a cohesive whole. It seemed to Romy that Dane was not in the theatre as often as he was before. He appeared content as well just to watch her from afar. All of which helped her sore heart to swell into even greater agony.

By Christmas, both her singles had made number one in the charts, and the duet by Mark and Simon was still steadily climbing. The advance bookings seemed to be breaking all records, and the press began their relentless interest in Dane's seeming change from his normal, successful formula into something so different. There were endless speculations about his reasons.

For quite long periods of time Romy completely forgot that Dane was supposedly working on her family problems; she even forgot them herself as she sank herself deeply into the part of 'Giselle'.

One dark afternoon, on looking into the stalls, she saw Dane, and sitting next to him, engrossed in conversation, was her cousin. Dane was bending forward to listen what she was saying, his dark head close, far too close, to the sleek blonde one.

Her worst fears were realised. Alone in her dressing-room, she changed into jeans and a thick, sloppy joe jumper. She didn't know whether to be furiously angry with herself for still harbouring hopes about Dane, or whether to cry her eyes out.

She heard one of the call-boys calling her name. 'Miss Brooke?'

'Yes?'

'Can you go to Mr Goodman's office right away?'

'Thank you!' She was due to see Lally Blair at her studio in three-quarters of an hour, that would just give her time to tell Mr Dane Goodman just exactly what she thought of him.

She left her room, determination and temper making her eyes flash dangerously as she made her way towards his office.

'Had a bad day?' Scotty enquired as Romy stopped in front of her desk, her navy-blue reefer jacket swinging from one of her fingers.

'You could say that!' Romy agreed grimly. 'Am I supposed to go straight in?' She didn't wait for an answer, just gave the jacket a final toss onto the chair in front of Scotty's desk, then opened the door to the inner office.

He was standing with his back to the door, and she could clearly see Elizabeth's hands clutching his shoulders as they exchanged a passionate kiss. Rage made it possible for her to close the door again, and pick up her coat. 'As you can see,' she said through gritted teeth, 'he's otherwise engaged!'

'Romy! Wait . . . It isn't what you think!'

'Are you asking me to deny what I saw with my own eyes?' she asked sweetly, before leaving the building in a rush.

There was a tiny, transport cafe tucked away in one of the side streets behind the theatre. Half-blinded by tears, Romy made her way to it and ordered a mug of hot, sweet tea which she carried to a table right at the back.

She wasn't dressed to attract attention so she was left to drink her tea in peace.

Elizabeth might have won the unacknowledged battle between them, but after this there was no way she would go along with Dane's plans. Why, he must have been seeing her cousin all the time, never breathing a word of it to her, the rat! She had given him the perfect opportunity to get to know Elizabeth. He knew how she felt about him, he always had . . . How could he have done this to her? He must have known that of all the women in the world to lose to, Elizabeth would be the most galling to her pride.

By the time she reached Lally's studio workroom she was suffering from an acute and corroding sense of disillusionment with the world. Even Lally, not usually the most observant of people unless it involved her work, had noticed it.

'Weather getting you down, Romy?'

'It's a foul time of year isn't it? I don't like the damp and cold . . . ' She hadn't the energy to really respond to anything but monosyllables after that.

She took a taxi home. The sight of Elizabeth, sitting and waiting for her in her house that maddened her all over again.

'How did you get in?' she demanded.

'Dane gave me a spare key . . . '

Romy had opened the door again. 'You and I have nothing to say to each other . . . '

'Please, Romy? Let me stay . . . We do have things to talk out and you know it!'

Romy pushed the door shut again, then took off her coat. 'All right, if you have to! But I warn you now, I'm tired, so don't take too long about it.' Her shoulders had slumped, as if she had acknowledged defeat. 'I'm going to make some tea, do you want some?'

'I'd love some! Can I help?'

'No, not really, I'll be out in a minute.'

She joined Elizabeth, balancing a tray with two mugs on it.

Elizabeth took a sip of tea. 'Why did you run out of Dane's office?'

'Be your age! Because it looked as if a third person would be totally unwelcome!'

'It wasn't what you thought, Romy! I've come here tonight because Dane was convinced he wouldn't get past your front door.'

'He was quite right, dear cousin!'

Elizabeth gave a rather theatrical sigh. 'Dane's been trying to sort out this mess over Gran's will, and he's come up with the idea that if we both have our debut the same night, then everything gets shared between us!'

Romy shrugged. 'Fine, in principle I suppose, but how's he going to pull it off?'

'Did you know he has an uncle who is in charge of the music at

Wellingborough Cathedral?' Romy gave a cautious nod. 'Well, he and Dane have written a Requiem Mass. Dane thinks it might have more impact if I take the lead role . . . Contadini is going to be conducting at the Albert Hall just three days before you are due to open, they're doing a piece by Verdi at the same time . . . Dane has arranged a special gala performance of 'Queen' for the same night, in aid of children's charities! He's already managed to get one 'royal' to attend . . . Don't you see, Romy? That way neither of us loses!'

'What does Uncle Max think of this?'

'Oh, he's thrilled of course, because it's the perfect answer. I thought it might have been fun if we both sang together, but Dane said that was impossible because you had too much to do with 'Queen', and I must say hearing you sing this afternoon, I have to agree with him! It's divine music, isn't it? And I guess quite difficult to sing, although you made it sound easy!'

Elizabeth gave her a worried look. 'You do agree, don't you?'

Romy felt as if her heart was bleeding inside her, but she rustled up a smile. 'I think it's the perfect solution as well . . . But isn't the publicity over 'Queen' going to slightly steal your thunder?'

'Oh no! Dane's going to put out a press release about Gran's will, and how we will both be making our debut on the same night!'

'I'm very happy for you, Elizabeth. Everything's worked out so well, thanks to Dane. You must be over the moon!'

'I am. Oh, I am! I never thought, until I met him, that there was any way of stopping this stupid feud between us. Now, we're both going to have successful careers, and I can forget my stupid jealousy about you!'

Romy was successfully diverted. 'Jealous? You?'

'Oh yes! I always knew you were going to be the better singer. Gran knew it too. She always believed in professional honesty. That's why she sounded a bit brutal at times. Anyway, as your career has taken a different direction, I can't see that mattering in the future, can you?'

'I don't know yet what I want to do, apart from singing 'Giselle', so I'll cross that bridge when I come to it,' Romy answered. 'Tell me what you have been doing. I thought you were with Southern Opera?'

'They are prepared to release me if I find something else to do.'

'Problems?' Romy queried.

'A soprano nearer fifty than forty who sees no reason why she shouldn't go on playing roles that are quite unsuited to her age and looks.'

'Oh dear!' Romy bit back a smile, 'but you should be used to that; think of Granny.'

'At least her voice was a great deal better. Anyway if I get this job in Munich, I shan't have to worry about her any more. Dane thinks he has enough contacts in the musical world to help me . . . I must say, he's quite some man, isn't he?' There was a roguish look in her eyes as she slid them towards to Romy. 'It'll be a lucky girl who manages to catch him, don't you think?'

'He's arrogant, demanding, and only interested in his music, as I'd have thought you'd have found out by now!'

Her cousin's eyes were shrewd, but she just smiled her small cat-like smile. 'I'd have thought it was almost impossible to resist those good looks, and think how rich he is!'

'It depends what you want out of life.'

'You're too like Gran, Romy! You've inherited all her guts, and I suppose we'll both do well enough not to need anyone's money but our own.'

'I hope so. I will probably set up a trust for struggling young singers when I get my share. She made all our lives a misery. If it hadn't been for her, maybe we could all have been friends.'

Elizabeth suddenly laughed rather harshly. 'I doubt it! In our different ways we're all too like her. I really admired her you know; she was always slightly larger than life, somehow, and although a tremendous egotist, when in good form could somehow make one catch fire from all that vitality she had.'

Romy sighed also. 'I didn't really like her, perhaps because of my mother . . . '

'You didn't like her because you recognised you were so like her.'

'Why,' Romy was surprised into complete naturalness, 'I believe you loved her!'

'Yes, I think perhaps I did, and I was the only one after her husband died . . . Daddy hated her quite as much as your mother did.'

Romy felt closer to her cousin in that moment than she ever had before. There would always be rivalry between them which would spur them both on to greater and greater heights. 'Good luck!' Romy said softly.

'Thanks, I shall need it!' Dane's

name lay unspoken between them, and Romy at that moment would have traded all her future success, everything, to have what she had discovered too late was the only thing she wanted. Elizabeth had won the only thing of importance.

It suddenly seemed right to her to relinquish all her dreams about Dane. A sacrifice on the altar of family stability if you like, but then he had never really been hers anyway. 'Not quite everything!' she answered Elizabeth drily, and knew her cousin understood her. 'Go and tell Dane that I agree to everything. Tell him also that for the moment I can only concentrate on 'Giselle'. He ought to understand; he told me himself there would be no room for any outside interests once I took her on!'

Her cousin needed Dane at the moment, far more than she did. Dane's strength would help her over the next few weeks. It would be a tragedy if one cousin should have a triumph greatly overshadowing the other. Whatever she might have said, Elizabeth had enough of her grandmother's determination to grasp her opportunity with both hands, and now she had Romy's blessing, so to speak, she would do so.

It seemed as if Dane understood her oblique message. He concerned himself only in his professional capacity with her performance, which she now immersed herself in, heart and soul.

Two weeks before the opening night, she came back to her dressing-room to find Scotty sitting there.

'This is a nice surprise! How are you?'

'I'm fine, and I think you are doing a terrific job on 'Giselle'.'

Romy could see that the older woman was slightly uncomfortable. 'Well, I can't believe you've come up here just to tell me that!'

'Dane wants to arrange a press conference with himself, Elizabeth and you!' she came out with, bluntly.

'Does he now?' Romy sat down at

the dressing-table.

'Yes. That way both of you will get maximum publicity, and he intends to tell the press about Dame Alicia's will, and how proud she would have been of you both!'

'I'm surprised he didn't come and ask me himself,' Romy remarked mildly.

Again, the older woman looked uncomfortable. 'I'm very sorry, Romy, I think he should have asked you himself.' She gave her a searching stare. 'Do you think you will be able to handle it? It's a good idea, but only if it doesn't worry you too much!'

'That's very nice of you, Scotty, but why should you think I would mind?'

'Because I know you are very fond of him, and I thought he felt the same way about you! I don't like him spending so much time with that cousin of yours! I can't think what he sees in her.'

Romy blindly put out a hand just to touch her. 'Thanks . . .'

'I blame myself!' Scotty continued, 'if only I'd checked before letting you walk into his office that day. He was terribly upset afterwards . . . Elizabeth is endlessly on the telephone to him, and I know he sees a lot of her.' Scotty blew her nose hard.

'Elizabeth needs help, maybe that's all it is!'

'I suppose so,' Scotty agreed, 'but she isn't making him happy, I do know that!'

Romy couldn't help a small ray of hope blossoming inside her, 'Perhaps he still hasn't got over Angie Tree!'

'Angela Tree? Whatever do you mean?'

'I was told he had been in love with her for years, and that is the reason he split with Eddie Linell!'

'Rubbish!' Scotty seemed to have recovered. 'More nonsense is talked in this business than any other. He's fond of Angela Tree, but there's never been anything serious between them, that I do know!'

'She's a very beautiful woman, all the same . . . ' It hurt Romy to say that, but it was the truth.

The older woman made a noise of disgust. 'Beautiful she may be, and talented, but there's never been anything but friendship between the two of them, whatever gossip might say!'

There was silence for a moment. 'Do you really think Dane was fond of me?' Romy asked wistfully.

'I'd have staked my life on it!' Scotty replied promptly. 'You didn't see what a state he was in when you were knocked down that night!' She got up to go, then with an air of throwing caution to the winds, turned again to Romy. 'Don't let him go without a fight! I don't really know what has gone wrong between you, but I think you are a fool to let your cousin walk in and take him over!'

# 9

Romy knew it would be impossible for her to meet Dane at the press conference without talking to him first to find out just how important his relationship with Elizabeth really was. If she was to face the eagle eyes of the press with equanimity, then she had to make sure she wasn't going to be thrown off balance by any dramatic announcement he might choose to make. She had heard too much gossip already from most of the cast of 'Queen' about Dane's supposed affair with her cousin.

Deep inside she believed he was only being kind to Elizabeth. However damped down she kept her feelings, she had always been aware of him with senses finely tuned to his physical presence, and in spite of everything, she thought he felt the same way.

Even if to him it was only a purely physical need, unimportant in any real sense, she sensed he would be unable to deny it because he had always been honest with her. Now she was secure and comfortable in her part as 'Giselle' or as much as she would ever be until the first night, she felt she could relax a little the guard she had put on her personal feelings. She had been able to discount most of the gossip from the cast because she knew they had no idea Dane was helping her cousin to arrange her concert and debut.

She was on the point of picking up the telephone, when she heard the doorbell. Sighing at the interruption, she uncurled herself from the sofa and opened the door.

She caught her breath at the shock of seeing Dane. 'I was just about to call you!' She stood aside to let him in.

She was amazed to notice that he looked a little uncomfortable, as if he wasn't at all sure what his welcome was going to be. She waited for him to speak, her eyebrows a little raised, a flicker of amusement in her eyes.

'Scotty seems to think I owe you a very big apology!' he told her, his mouth twisted ruefully. He produced a bottle of champagne from under his coat. 'I thought we could drink some of this, then I'll take you out to dinner, always supposing you're not already going out?'

'You know perfectly well I never go out during the week!'

'Does that mean you won't come out with me tonight?'

'Actually I'd love to go out! It's ages since I've been anywhere except home and the theatre . . . '

'I warned you, didn't I, that life would be tough?'

'Indeed you did, about that and other things too!' She moved towards the kitchen. 'You open the bottle, and I'll get the glasses.' She felt suddenly supremely alive and happy, 'and when you've given me my glass I'll go up and change!'

He laughed at her when she came back with the glasses. 'Don't put on anything too exotic, or I'll have to go home and change as well!' He opened the bottle with a satisfying plop.

It didn't take Romy long to change. She had already had a bath and she decided that she would wear black. A soft wool dress with a demure neckline and three-quarter length sleeves, teamed with black wool tights. The final effect looked a bit sombre, so she tied a gaily patterned shawl round her shoulders.

Satisfied at last with her appearance, she went down to join Dane.

He was at his attentive and charming best all through dinner at the discreet and expensive restaurant where he had taken her. Obviously very well known by the staff, she couldn't help wondering who else he brought here as his companion. As if by common consent their conversation was light and entertaining on the surface, but deeper down, a more profound communication was taking place between them. The sexual excitement between them grew stronger, as if this time it wouldn't be denied.

His hand closed over hers in the car and removed the key of the little house from her fingers. Once they were both inside, he kicked the door shut and pulled her into his arms, his mouth seeking hers with an urgency and delight that had her responding like a flower to the sun.

'O God!' he said later, 'I've wanted to do that for months!'

'Why didn't you then?' she teased.

'Because you . . . ' he cupped her face with his hands, 'made it all too clear that you didn't want me to!'

'I did?' she protested indignantly, 'I certainly did not! You were the one who told me there wouldn't be time for any boyfriends if I took on 'Giselle'!'

'Yes, but I didn't mean you to include me!'

'Didn't you?' She was suddenly shy, 'I wish I'd known that!'

He gave an incredulous laugh, and pulled her hard against him. His voice sounded slightly slurred with passion as he said, 'I want you, Romy! I've wanted you in my bed for months, ever since that disastrous fiasco at Grâcedieu . . . I knew, or thought I knew that you felt the same way about me, then I began to have doubts. Perhaps you didn't feel as I did. Maybe you were just using me to further your career. Believe me, you've had me tied up in such knots that it's been a miracle I've been able to work at all!' His mouth sought hers again and she strove to make him forget any doubts he might still have about her.

He moved his lips from hers with obvious difficulty. 'Listen, sweetheart, we have to talk . . . ' He picked her up and carried her over to the sofa, sitting down with her still cradled in his arms. Her hands were gently exploring the contours of his head, her fingers relishing the feel of his dark, springing hair, so vibrant with life under her touch. 'O God, no!' His hands caught her arms, imprisoning them. 'How can I think when you do that?' he groaned.

His hands slid up under her skirt. 'You've got too many clothes on . . . ' She could feel his skin burning with desire, and her own rose in an overwhelming wave to meet it. 'You are so very beautiful . . . ' his hands traced trembling, impatient patterns on her skin, his fingers having already expertly removed the thick, wool tights, his mouth once again seeking and finding hers to plunder its sweet depths.

Voluptuously she allowed delicious anticipation to hold her in thrall as he slowly removed her dress, then her bra, before his mouth sought the hard, rosy peaks of her breasts. Deep throbbing pleasure filled her as his mouth closed over hers, having her arching towards him, her head thrown back as she moaned with delight under his sure touch.

'O Dane . . . please . . . ' She didn't

consciously know what she begged for, but it seemed as if he did, as one hand slid slowly down, seeking the velvet smoothness of her inner thigh. As he found then touched the source of her delight, she moaned again, beyond feeling anything but the pleasure he could give her. Nothing else mattered, nothing, except that this heaven should go on and on . . .

His hand stilled, then moved away, and she became irritatingly aware that the phone was ringing.

'Don't answer it, please?' she buried herself against him, her arms entwined round his neck.

'I must, my darling . . . I left this number with Scotty for emergencies, unless it's someone for you?'

'No-one I know would ring me this late . . . ' she protested.

He stopped her mouth with a quick kiss before picking up the phone. 'Yes?' A dark frown drew his heavy brows together. 'What?'

Romy strained to hear the voice at

the other end, but was forced to admit defeat. Dane still held her close to him, one hand playing idly with her breasts, but suddenly impatient, she moved away. She ran lightly up the stairs to the bathroom and becoming aware of her nakedness, pulled her robe round her. The mirror showed her a face quite different from her normal one; her eyes looked twice as big, her cheeks flushed.

She smiled at herself, before picking up her hair-brush to tidy her hair. She moved into the bedroom, pulling off the bedcover, before getting into bed.

She heard his voice calling her name, and his feet lightly running up the stairs. She snuggled down into the pillows, waiting for him to come and find her. The only lamp was the small one by her bed, its light intimate, filling the rest of the room with shadows.

'Romy?' Dane came into the room, and she heard his quickly indrawn breath as he looked at her. 'Oh God!' She was in no doubt about the anguish she heard in his voice.

'What is it? What's happened?' She sat up hurriedly, uncaring that the light gave her skin a rosy glow all of its own, as her nakedness was revealed.

'I've got to go . . . ' his voice sounded strangled, 'it's Elizabeth, she's in trouble . . . '

'Elizabeth?' Her voice rose in crescendo. 'You're leaving me now because Elizabeth wants you?' The tears were pouring down her face. 'How could you do this to me? You know just how important . . . ' She was shaken by a convulsive sob.

'Romy! For God's sake, do you think I want to leave?'

'If I was important to you, you'd stay! Please?' She held out one hand, palm upward, in supplication.

He shut his eyes. 'I can't! Tomorrow you'll know why . . . Trust me, Romy, I beg of you!'

She gave a great hiccuping sob, but her eyes were fierce as they tried to probe his shadowy face. 'If you walk out on me now, with no explanation, then it's finished, do you understand?'

He looked suddenly very tired. 'I'm sorry . . . I wish you could have trusted me, but perhaps as you can't, then it's better we both have nothing to regret, isn't it? I won't bother you again . . . ' Romy waited until he had left the room before crying her eyes out.

She was sitting miserably in her room at the theatre the next day, when her eyes was caught by a small paragraph in the paper she was reading.

'A tragic accident,' she read, 'happened yesterday evening. Mr Maximilian Hepburn, only son of the late Dame Alicia Hepburn, was severely wounded in a small explosion which took place in his house. It is not known what caused the accident. Mr Hepburn is the father of Elizabeth Hepburn who is due to make her debut as a solo singer next week at a concert in the Albert Hall, conducted by Mr Arturo Contadini.'

Romy read the paragraph again with an increasing sense of shock. Why on earth hadn't Dane told her last night? Without stopping to think, she left her dressing-room heading for Dane's office.

Scotty's room was empty, surprisingly, but through the half-shut door to Dane's room she heard his voice raised in anger.

'I can't see why she should be told this! She would find it extremely upsetting as well as distressing, and she's playing the lead role in a show which is due to open in less than ten days. Do you want to upset her, now?'

Romy decided she had heard enough. She pushed the door open and walked in. Elizabeth, looking white and pale, was sitting in a chair with Scotty standing over her. Two other men were standing in a group by Dane in front of the window.

Elizabeth's cry of 'Romy!' alerted them to her presence. Dane reacted quickly, coming and putting an arm around her shoulders. 'You've heard then?' he queried in quick sympathy.

'Miss Brooke? I'm Detective Sergeant Richards, investigating an accident that took place at Mr Maximilian Hepburn's house yesterday evening. We would like to question you about one or two matters concerning it.'

'For heaven's sake!' Dane interrupted sharply, 'not in front of Miss Hepburn . . . '

'All right sir . . . May we use another room?'

'No! Scotty, can you look after Elizabeth please? I'll stay here with Romy.'

Elizabeth left the room, giving Romy a look of agonised appeal, that brought a puzzled frown to her face. Dane still had his arm around her. 'Come and sit down, darling! This may be a bit of a shock for you . . . ' He gave one shoulder a warning squeeze before moving away from her.

Romy was therefore braced for trouble, but what the sergeant told her almost shattered her. 'We have reason to believe, Miss Brooke, that Mr

Hepburn was injured trying to construct a parcel bomb addressed to you!'

'What?'

Dane moved over quickly to take one of her hands in a warm clasp. 'Elizabeth and I have been trying to tell the sergeant for hours that the whole idea is impossible . . . '

'But of course the whole idea's impossible!' Romy agreed. 'Why on earth should you think he would do anything like that?'

'We have been given to understand that he grudged you your share under your grandmother's will!'

Romy shook her head violently. 'Oh, no! He would have been upset, of course, if I inherited it all, but there is no question of that . . . He was delighted when he heard that both his daughter and I would benefit equally . . . '

'I understand you parted on rather bad terms?'

Romy made her face look a little puzzled. 'Who on earth could have

198

told you that? On the contrary, when my parents died, he offered me a room in his house . . . ' She was silent for a moment. 'I wanted to pursue my career so that's why I didn't live there.'

'Miss Brooke, this is a very serious matter. Are you absolutely sure that your uncle had no grudge against you?'

She managed to look surprised. 'I don't know him terribly well, I agree, because not surprisingly he's been more interested in Elizabeth's career than mine . . . After all she is the one who is most closely following his mother's footsteps!'

The sergeant questioned her closely about her uncle's interest in model engineering but it soon became clear to him that Romy couldn't or wouldn't be persuaded to say anything against her uncle.

'Oh my darling!' Dane gathered her into his arms as soon as they were alone. 'I would have given anything in the world to have spared you that ordeal . . . '

'Uncle Max?' she whispered into his shoulder.

'Not very good, sweetheart, which I suppose is a blessing. They don't expect him to live more than a few hours, so that's why the charade . . . '

'I understand.' She held him tightly against her.

'If anything had happened to you . . . ' he shuddered violently, 'I would have had to blame myself for the rest of my life! I never dreamed he still felt that way about you . . . '

'What about Elizabeth, does she believe it?'

'I don't know . . . I hope that once he dies she will make herself think it was only an accident. She owes you so much, my darling, and you've been so generous to her, to me . . . You've had a very poor return for your kindness so far, haven't you?' He tipped her face up to his. 'I love you Romy, more than I would ever have believed I could love any woman! I want you to marry me, and I'll spend the rest of my life trying

200

to make you happy. We'll make music together my darling, music so beautiful that everyone will know how I feel about you!' He kissed her lightly on the lips. 'Well, are you still going to punish me for walking out on you last night?'

'You ever do that to me again . . . ' but he didn't allow her to finish, just kissed her hard instead.

'We'll announce our engagement before the opening night, shall we?' he teased. 'I'm not an accomplished actor my darling; everyone will be able to guess exactly what I'm feeling . . . Come on, we have some unfinished business . . . '

'What about Elizabeth?' she protested.

'There's nothing either of us can do to help her at this moment,' he answered soberly. 'Scotty will take care of her, and she understands about us . . . She's always known I intended to ask you to marry me . . . '

She gave a sigh of pure happiness and gave him a hug before they drove home together.

★ ★ ★

Romy sat in the dressing-room listening over the tannoy to the audience settling into their seats. On her dressing-table was a single white gardenia from her cousin. She had sent exactly the same token to her. Dame Alicia had always had a white gardenia sent to her on her opening night. An enormous basket of red roses from Dane were the only other flowers she had allowed in the room.

Mo, her dresser, fidgeted around behind her, checking on her different changes. There was an air of intense, if suppressed excitement about her. 'Feeling all right, ducks?' she enquired. Romy smiled and nodded at her in the mirror, still busy putting the finishing touches to her make-up. Dane had been in to see her earlier, but was wise enough not to distract her too long from the most important moment in her career so far.

There were butterflies in her tummy,

but she knew she could do it. Tonight would be a shared triumph for both Dane and herself, as well as Luke Seaward and the rest of the cast.

'Overture and beginners please! Overture and beginners please!'

She stood up while Mo gave the dress some last minute twitches, then left the room to take her place in the wings. She heard the familiar music, then forgot everything except that she was 'Giselle' a nightclub singer going out to meet her love.

As the final curtain fell, there was an uncanny silence, then a roar of applause, as deafening as a tidal wave, and almost as overwhelming to her. There were tears in her eyes as she ran to the wings and Dane's arms. They closed round her tightly. 'Thank you, my darling,' he whispered, then let her go, for the first of her innumerable curtain calls of the most memorable night of her life.

# Other titles in the
# Linford Romance Library

## SAVAGE PARADISE
### Sheila Belshaw

For four years, Diana Hamilton had dreamed of returning to Luangwa Valley in Zambia. Now she was back — and, after a close encounter with a rhino — was receiving a lecture from a tall, khaki-clad man on the dangers of going into the bush alone!

## PAST BETRAYALS
### Giulia Gray

As soon as Jon realized that Julia had fallen in love with him, he broke off their relationship and returned to work in the Middle East. When Jon's best friend, Danny, proposed a marriage of friendship, Julia accepted. Then Jon returned and Julia discovered her love for him remained unchanged.

## PRETTY MAIDS ALL IN A ROW
### Rose Meadows

The six beautiful daughters of George III of England dreamt of handsome princes coming to claim them, but the King always found some excuse to reject proposals of marriage. This is the story of what befell the Princesses as they began to seek lovers at their father's court, leaving behind rumours of secret marriages and illegitimate children.


## THE GOLDEN GIRL
### Paula Lindsay

Sarah had everything — wealth, social background, great beauty and magnetic charm. Her heart was ruled by love and compassion for the less fortunate in life. Yet, when one man's happiness was at stake, she failed him — and herself.

## A DREAM OF HER OWN
### Barbara Best
A stranger gently kisses Sarah Danbury at her Betrothal Ball. Little does she realise that she is to meet this mysterious man again in very different circumstances.

## HOSTAGE OF LOVE
### Nara Lake
From the moment pretty Emma Tregear, the only child of a Van Diemen's Land magnate, met Philip Despard, she was desperately in love. Unfortunately, handsome Philip was a convict on parole.

## THE ROAD TO BENDOUR
### Joyce Eaglestone
Mary Mackenzie had lived a sheltered life on the family farm in Scotland. When she took a job in the city she was soon in a romantic maze from which only she could find the way out.

## NEW BEGINNINGS
### Ann Jennings
On the plane to his new job in a hospital in Turkey, Felix asked Harriet to put their engagement on hold, as Philippe Krir, the Director of Bodrum hospital, refused to hire 'attached' people. But, without an engagement ring, what possible excuse did Harriet have for holding Philippe at bay?


## THE CAPTAIN'S LADY
### Rachelle Edwards
1820: When Lianne Vernon becomes governess at Elswick Manor, she finds her young pupil is given to strange imaginings and that her employer, Captain Gideon Lang, is the most enigmatic man she has ever encountered. Soon Lianne begins to fear for her pupil's safety.

## THE VAUGHAN PRIDE
### Margaret Miles
As the new owner of Southwood Manor, Laura Vaughan discovers that she's even more poverty stricken than before. She also finds that her neighbour, the handsome Marius Kerr, is a little too close for comfort.

## HONEY-POT
### Mira Stables
Lovely, well-born, well-dowered, Russet Ingram drew all men to her. Yet here she was, a prisoner of the one man immune to her graces — accused of frivolously tampering with his young ward's romance!

## DREAM OF LOVE
### Helen McCabe
When there is a break-in at the art gallery she runs, Jade can't believe that Corin Bossinney is a trickster, or that she'd fallen for the oldest trick in the book . . .

## FOR LOVE OF OLIVER
### Diney Delancey

When Oliver Scott buys her family home, Carly retains the stable block from which she runs her riding school. But she soon discovers Oliver is not an easy neighbour to have. Then Carly is presented with a new challenge, one she must face for love of Oliver.


## THE SECRET OF MONKS' HOUSE
### Rachelle Edwards

Soon after her arrival at Monks' House, Lilith had been told that it was haunted by a monk, and she had laughed. Of greater interest was their neighbour, the mysterious Fabian Delamaye. Was he truly as debauched as rumour told, and what was the truth about his wife's death?

## THE SPANISH HOUSE
### Nancy John

Lynn couldn't help falling in love with the arrogant Brett Sackville. But Brett refused to believe that she felt nothing for his half-brother, Rafael. Lynn knew that the cruel game Brett made her play to protect Rafael's heart could end only by breaking hers.


## PROUD SURGEON
### Lynne Collins

Calder Savage, the new Senior Surgical Officer at St. Antony's Hospital, had really lived up to his name, venting a savage irony on anyone who fell foul of him. But when he gave Staff Nurse Honor Portland a lift home, she was surprised to find what an interesting man he was.

## A PARTNER FOR PENNY
### Pamela Forest

Penny had grown up with Christopher Lloyd and saw in him the older brother she'd never had. She was dismayed when he was arrogantly confident that she should not trust her new business colleague, Gerald Hart. She opposed Chris by setting out to win Gerald as a partner both in love and business.

## SURGEON ASHORE
### Ann Jennings

Luke Roderick, the new Consultant Surgeon for Accident and Emergency, couldn't understand why Staff Nurse Naomi Selbourne refused to apply for the vacant post of Sister. Naomi wasn't about to tell him that she moonlighted as a waitress in order to support her small nephew, Toby.

# A MOONLIGHT MEETING
## Peggy Gaddis

Megan seemed to have fallen under handsome Tom Fallon's spell, and she was no longer sure if she would be happy as Larry's wife. It was only in the aftermath of a terrible tragedy that she realized the true meaning of love.

# THE STARLIT GARDEN
## Patricia Hemstock

When interior designer Tansy Donaghue accepted a commission to restore Beechwood Manor in Devon, she was relieved to leave London and its memories of her broken romance with architect Robert Jarvis. But her dream of a peaceful break was shattered not only by Robert's unexpected visit, but also by the manipulative charms of the manor's owner, James Buchanan.

## THE BECKONING DAWN
### Georgina Ferrand

For twenty-five years Caroline has lived the life of a recluse, believing she is ugly because of a facial scar. After a successful operation, the handsome Anton Tessler comes into her life. However, Caroline soon learns that the kind of love she yearns for may never be hers.

## THE WAY OF THE HEART
### Rebecca Marsh

It was the scandal of the season when world-famous actress Andrea Lawrence stalked out of a Broadway hit to go home again. But she hadn't jeopardized her career for nothing. The beautiful star was onstage for the play of her life — a drama of double-dealing romance starring her sister's fiancé.

## VIENNA MASQUERADE
### Lorna McKenzie

In Austria, Kristal Hastings meets Rodolfo von Steinberg, the young cousin of Baron Gustav von Steinberg, who had been her grandmother's lover many years ago. An instant attraction flares between them — but how can Kristal give her love to Rudi when he is already promised to another . . . ?

## HIDDEN LOVE
### Margaret McDonagh

Until his marriage, Matt had seemed like an older brother to Teresa. Now, five years later, Matt's wife has tragically died and Teresa feels she must go and comfort him. But how much longer can she hold on to the secret that has been hers for all these years?

# A MOST UNUSUAL MARRIAGE
## Barbara Best

Practically penniless, Dorcas Wareham meets Suzette, who tells her that she had rashly married a Captain Jack Bickley on the eve of his leaving for the Boer War. She suggests that Dorcas takes her place, saying that Jack didn't expect to survive the war anyway. With some misgivings, Dorcas finally agrees. But Jack does return . . .

# A TOUCH OF TENDERNESS
## Juliet Gray

Ben knew just how to charm, how to captivate a woman — though he could not win a heart that was already in another man's keeping. But Clare was desperately anxious to protect him from a pain she knew too well herself.

## NEED FOR A NURSE
### Lynne Collins

When Kelvin, a celebrated actor, regained consciousness after a car accident, he had lost his memory. He was shocked to learn that he was engaged to the beautiful actress Beth Hastings. His mind was troubled — and so was his heart when he became aware of the impact on his emotions of a pretty staff nurse . . .

## WHISPER OF DOUBT
### Rachel Croft

Fiona goes to Culvie Castle to value paintings for the owner, who is in America. After meeting Ewen McDermott, the heir to the castle, Fiona suspects that there is something suspicious going on. But little does she realise what heartache lies ahead of her . . .

## MISTRESS AT THE HALL
### Eileen Knowles
Sir Richard Thornton makes Gina welcome at the Hall, but his grandson, Zachary, calls her a fortune hunter. After Sir Richard's death, Gina finds taking over the role of Mistress at the Hall far from easy, and Zachary doesn't help — until he realises that he loves her.


## PADLOCK YOUR HEART
### Anne Saunders
Ignoring James Thornton's warning that it was cruel to give false hope, Faith set up a fund to send little Debby to Russia for treatment. Despite herself, Faith found she was falling in love with James. Perhaps she should have padlocked her heart against him.

## AN UNEQUAL MATCH
### Rachelle Edwards

Penniless and hungry, it seems that life could not be worse for Verena — until her father secures a marriage for her to the new Marquis of Strafford. Filled with disgust at this urchin, the Marquis leaves for France the day after the ceremony. But when he returns after two years, the situation is vastly different . . .

## ASSIGNMENT IN VENICE
### Georgina Ferrand

Freelance photographer Rhia Stacey was given the once-in-a-lifetime opportunity to collaborate on a book about Venice with the Marchesa di Stefano. But Rhia discovered an attraction to the Marchese Dario di Stefano, which could only lead to heartache.